"You still wear your wedding ring?"

"It adds protection. Why would I not?"

She looked at him in a hard and direct way as she said it, and he thought how seldom she smiled anymore.

"I can protect you." The fever burned and his thigh throbbed, but he meant what he promised. War had changed her, but it had changed him, too.

"I have no more need of a man's guardianship, Major."

"No?" He took the hand without the ring and turned it over. Breathing out, he tried the taste of honesty. "It seems to me as though you do."

SOPHIA JAMES

—

A Night of Secret Surrender

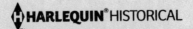
HARLEQUIN® HISTORICAL

Recycling programs
for this product may
not exist in your area.

ISBN-13: 978-1-335-05171-4

A Night of Secret Surrender

Printed in U.S.A.

www.Harlequin.com

Sophia James lives in Chelsea Bay, on the North Shore of Auckland, New Zealand, with her husband, who is an artist. She has a degree in English and history from Auckland University and believes her love of writing was formed by reading Georgette Heyer on vacations at her grandmother's house. Sophia enjoys getting feedback at Facebook.com/sophiajamesauthor.

Visit the Author Profile page
at Harlequin.com for more titles.

I'd like to dedicate this book to my wonderful mother, Jewell Kivell. She's always been one of the greatest supporters of my writing and I miss her.

Author Note

Paris in 1812 was a city full of factions vying for political influence. Napoleon Bonaparte had departed from France to take the Grande Armée into Russia, leaving a power vacuum in his wake. Two men more than happy to extend their authority were Henri Jacques Guillaume Clarke, the Minister of War, and Anne Jean Marie René Savary, the newly appointed Minister of Police.

Clarke was particularly good at encroaching upon weaker men and ministries, and in the absence of the Emperor he extended his considerable authority even further. A Frenchman of Irish descent, he was known as a wily opponent with the sort of cleverness that worried even Napoleon. But by the end of the year he would fall from favour.

The Ministry of Police had been set up by Joseph Fouché and, although Savary had the running of the ministry in 1812, Fouché's omnipresence and calculated cunning was instilled into the culture.

Beneath the larger official ministries, smaller intelligence agencies flourished and it is here I have fashioned the fictional Les Chevaliers, of which my heroine Celeste Fournier is a part.

France in 1812 was at war with Britain, but America, under President Madison, had sent envoys to Paris to test the waters, so to speak.

The time was ripe for change and everyone wanted the chance to lead France into the new century. An Empire at risk made things in the country that much more volatile—the perfect place to set a story.

Chapter One

Paris, France—June 1812

Major Summerley Shayborne opened the door to his accommodation on the Rue St Denis to find a young woman waiting inside among the evening shadows.

She wore thick glasses and her pure white hair was fastened loosely at her nape. He had not seen such a colour on anyone of her age before and so could only imagine it false.

'I am here to warn you, *monsieur.*'

Shay saw the sheen of a blade in her left hand before it was slipped away out of sight.

'Warn me of what, *madame*?' He could not place her accent; the French she spoke was tinged with the cadence of one who did not belong anywhere.

'Savary and the Ministry of Police are watching you.' Her diction was precise as she continued talking. 'You have held too many conversations about French military affairs on the Champs de Mars and in the coffee houses, and people are beginning to ask their questions.'

Lighting a candle, she turned away, shielding herself from the brightness. As the flame took, she allowed it to illuminate him instead, the planes of her own face left in semi-darkness.

'It is even being inferred that you might not be an American officer at all.'

'Who are you?'

She laughed quickly at that, though the sound held little humour and he felt a sudden slide of cold running down his back.

'Politics here takes no prisoners. One wrong move and you will be dead. Even a charming and inquisitive foreigner is not immune to a knife quietly slipped between your ribs.' Her stillness was amplified by the movement of flame. 'The police bureau will be here within days, asking their questions. You are a spy, Major Shayborne, of immeasurable value to both sides, but there always comes a time when luck simply runs out.'

The shock of her words had him turning.

'Why would you tell me this?'

'History,' she whispered and walked to the door, opening it with care before slipping out into the oncoming dark.

Shay did not move, rooted to the spot in sudden comprehension of what she had said.

History.

There was something familiar in the timbre of her voice beneath the accent, under the hard anger, behind the thick lenses and hidden by a false wig. A memory.

Like an echo in the blood. He stood as still as he could, trying to reach out and claim it.

She moved through the roads leading to the Palais Royale with a practised ease and up through the alleyways to the Rue de Petit Champs, walking quickly but not too fast, for such speed would draw attention. It was a warm night for June, the oncoming heat of summer felt through the grates and on the cobbles and the south-facing walls. Her hand ran across the patinas of chalky sand and limestone. Ahead she saw the tavern she sometimes stopped at was alive with people. Melting into the shadows, she brought the hood of her silken cape up, the new and expensive white wig stuffed into her pocket because it was too noticeable.

She did not wish to see anyone tonight and have to explain herself. She wanted to wash. She wanted to sit on her balcony and have a glass of the smoky Pouilly-Fumé she had bought yesterday in the Marais from the Jewish shopkeeper with good contacts in the fertile, grape-bearing valleys of the Loire.

She wanted to be alone.

She should have sent someone else to warn Shayborne. She could have penned a note or whispered her message in the darkness without lighting the candle. She could have transferred her information by any number of safe and practical methods, but she had not. She had gone to see him and whispered exactly what she should have kept to herself.

History.

One word coated in shame and blood. One word that

had taken her from the girl she had been to the woman she had become.

She'd shown her hand because the Police Ministry and the War Office would soon be as much on her tail as they were on Shayborne's and because after six years on the run she had finally exhausted all options.

It would be a miracle if she was not dead before him even, this English spy who had the whole of France in an uproar after his escape in Bayonne and who, instead of turning back to Spain and safety as he'd been expected to, had made his way north to the very heart of Napoleon's lair.

Why?

She knew the reason even as she asked it.

He was here to understand what might happen next and where the Emperor would employ his might: Russia or the Continent, the size of amassing armies. Information like that could change the course of a war and the British General, Arthur Wellesley, waited in the wings of the northern Spanish coast for a direction.

Once she might have cared more, might have turned her ear to the rumblings of the generals or the whining of the various ministries and listened well.

But there was only so much truth one could discover before the lies ate you up. Deceit had its limits and hers were almost reached, here in a city she no longer could call her own.

She'd made the mistake of entrusting sensitive documents to a courier who she now knew was playing her false and the larger part of a family had died because of it. She could not quite understand yet how this betrayal had happened. Someone else higher up had given orders for the demise of the Dubois family, but it was her name splattered all over the debacle, her reputation, her life hanging by a thread in the aftermath of murder. Those who had died had been good people, innocent people, people without knowledge of the terrible depth a festering war could be taken to, people in the wrong place at the wrong time and two of them had been children. The horror of it consumed her.

Sometimes, for no reason at all, her heart beat so fast she thought she might simply fall down with the breathlessness of it, hatred caught in her throat like a fishbone.

Swearing, she sifted through the pathways still open to her. She couldn't go back to England even had she wanted to. She would need to disappear and become someone else entirely, but first she needed to see that what was left of the Dubois family was taken to safety. She owed them at least that and the money she'd earned from trading secrets was in a place readily accessible. It could be done.

The ports were shut and barricaded and any traveller moving great distances was watched. Still, she could slink like a shadow through any city in Europe and once outside the limits of Paris she would not be known.

She frowned at this. She also knew that she could not leave Major Shayborne at the mercy of all those who would want to kill him. She'd been astonished when she had seen that it was indeed he as he had entered his lodgings. After all these years, she had not expected ever to lay eyes upon him again and certainly not in the heart of his enemy's territory.

His eyes were more golden than she remembered and his face was leaner. His hair was dark-dyed, she was sure of it, but time had been kinder to him than it had been to her.

'A shame, that,' she whispered, knowing betrayal lined her forehead with its bitter recriminations and surprising violence.

Once, she had been beautiful, too, when she had first come here with her father from England eight years ago, but she shook away that sadness and concentrated on the pathway home. Through La Place de La Bourse and the quiet sombreness of the first arrondissement to the Rue St Berger. Here the buildings were less embellished and less grand and the streets were narrower. A dog barked and she stood still a moment, waiting for it to cease, pausing for the breeze to blow between them before creeping more silently up the circular steps. Another set of stairs and the doorway to her room was before her. She checked the lock and saw the fine, unbroken strand of hair still attached to it. The light dust she had scattered on her step was unmarked, too, and so slipping in the key she went inside.

The darkness. The silence. Closing her eyes in relief, she retraced her journey the way she always did, every single night of her return.

No one had followed her. The shadows from the lanterns had remained unbroken and the narrow arches of Les Halles, with the circular Halle aux Blés at its western edge, had been empty of threat. The smaller throughways had held no detected dangers, nor had the brighter Rue de Louvre.

This was her home now, this small part of Paris, and she knew it like the back of her hand—every face, every stone, every sound of every moving entity. Such knowledge afforded her protection and brought with it an inevitable isolation, but she was used to being alone.

Inside her rooms there was very little. It was how she liked it. It was how she had lived for all those weeks and months and years since her father had been murdered. It was the way she had survived after being thrown into chaos.

History.

She should not have whispered such a word, but underneath it was another truth that had wound across a shallow vanity and shown itself. She'd seen the flicker of it in his eyes.

In her dreams she'd known it, too.

What could Shayborne do with such information anyway, for he had only a matter of days to leave? Celeste held her breath with the shock of seeing him. None save Jules, her contact in the War Office, had figured out just who he was yet, but it was only a matter of making connections and those agents trying to find Shayborne would see all that they had missed.

She'd paid Jules well to buy his silence for forty-eight hours, but realistically she could expect no more than twenty-four. Such a secret was worth a small fortune and the agent would be weighing allegiances against cold, hard cash. Perhaps even twelve hours might be asking too much?

McPherson was a suspect, too, the old Scottish jeweller trawling to ascertain the truth of Napoleon's movements in a way that did not raise suspicion at first…

Put them together and anyone would have him, Lord Summerley Anthony William Shayborne. Summer. She had called him that. The name rolled across her tongue and she swallowed away the taste of it. He was no longer hers. They had both been dealt hands that had torn them apart for ever, changing them beyond recognition from the innocents they'd once been.

Opening the curtain, she slipped out on to the balcony, making certain to stay against the wall. She seldom stood in the open any more for it was dangerous to be caught in the light. There was always something firm at her back, something solid and thick and protective.

With care, she undid her cloak and loosened the ties of her bodice, letting the night caress her skin. Her nipples stood proud at their release and she laid her head back and closed her eyes.

Remembering.

The feel of him against her, his care and his heat, taut and solid. She had thought of these things after her father had died and she had been taken. Then, only the memory of Shayborne's goodness and honour had saved her, for the way he had said her name in the night under the softer stars of Sussex had felt like music and the feel of him inside her like a song. She'd always sensed the danger in him, too, honed by a civic duty, but crouching close. The violence and the stillness, side by side, a heady combination that had drawn her to him. He was a man who might triumph over every obstacle thrown his way and live.

'Notre Père, qui est aux cieux…'

The age-old words of the Lord's Prayer soothed her and she fumbled in her pocket for her father's rosary, fingers sliding over polished amber with easy practice.

Lying with Summer was one action she had never regretted, not then and not now. She could remember the girl she'd been, the innocence as well as the arrogance. Did all young, beautiful women behave in such a dreadfully entitled fashion, or was it just her? Well, no longer, at least.

She looked down and saw the scars on her left wrist, pale white and faded. One finger traced the lines, the numbness there still surprising. This was who she had become, this damaged person who understood the true extent of terror and who had survived. Just.

She wished she had not cut her hair so short. The bluntness of the shorn ends made it prickle around her face.

Lifting up the glass of fine Pouilly-Fumé, she swallowed the lot and helped herself to another, her anxieties lessening.

Shay closed the curtains before lighting two other candles and placing them on each side of the mantel.

He was tired of Paris, tired of its subterfuge and its darkness. He'd realised who his visitor was within minutes of her leaving.

Celeste Fournier. It had been eight years since he had seen her last in England. She'd been lauded for her beauty by all who had met her, but it was the broken pieces that he had loved the most, the vulnerable parts she'd hidden under a smile.

Loved? Too strong a word perhaps, though at eighteen the heart was inclined to excess.

Another knock at the door had him turning. Could she have come back? Unlocking the bolts, he found Richard Cunningham on his step and shut the door quickly behind him, Celeste's recent warning ringing in his head.

'You look like you have seen a ghost, Rick?'

'Perhaps I have.' The newcomer could not quite keep the worry from his words as he crossed over to the table and helped himself to a drink. Brandy and his best bottle. Cunningham's taste was impeccable even under duress.

'There are problems afoot, Shay. A fracas yesterday has ripped apart the private world of Parisian intelligence and each office is blaming the others in their various bids for more power. As a result, it is now every man for himself and a dagger in the back is a very real concern.'

'You are speaking of the murder of the Dubois family?'

'You've heard of it, then? From whom?' His friend's dark eyes widened. 'Word on the street has it that Napoleon's agencies are exterminating anyone who fails to agree with the Emperor's vision for France. That includes the families of those who might have the temerity to criticise a regime that many know is tainted. They were said to be in receipt of incriminating documents, papers which raised questions about their loyalty to France. Napoleon has gone mad with his greed for power!'

'Threads,' Shay returned, 'threads bound and winding into the foolish hope of greatness. Conquer Russia and nobody will be able to stop Bonaparte from ruling the world.'

'It will be winter that brings him to his knees, mark my words. There are thousands and thousands of miles between here and Moscow.'

'So you are leaving? Getting out?' Shay's eyes dropped to a bag near the door.

'I am. Tonight. Come with me. It's the only option that makes sense.'

Fifteen minutes ago Shay thought he might have done just that. A quarter of an hour ago, he might have packed his bag summarily and left the city, his reports completed, his duties done.

But now he shook his head. 'There is something I still have to finish.'

He thought of Celeste. He thought of her gift to him in the hay barn at Langley, the winter sun slanting through the dirty glass of a cracked window. Long limbed, perfect and sad.

'Does James McPherson know of the danger?' There were others to be considered, too.

'If he doesn't, the channels of his intelligence are failing him. It's over here, don't you see? There is nothing left that could make a difference to the outcome of a war that defies every tenet of sense. If the Little General wants to cut his own throat, then who are we to hang around and bathe in the blood of it?'

'Which way are you headed?'

'To the coast in the north. There are fishermen whom I wager would place gold above the sway of politics if given the chance and will transport me across the channel.'

'Then I wish you good luck and God speed.'

'You won't come?'

'I think you will have a better chance of safety without me. My cover here has been blown. I heard of this today.'

'God. Then why the hell are you staying?'

'It's just for a little while. I will leave tomorrow night.'

'Find another uniform, then. I've heard rumours that every American envoy of President Madison will be searched.'

'I have already heard that warning, but thank you.'

'There's a brandy waiting for you in a London pub when you make it home.'

'I'll hold you to it.'

'You're a hero, Shay, in Spain and in England, but be mindful that you only live once.'

'And die once?'

'That, too.'

When he was gone, Shay crossed the room and finished the cognac that Cunningham had poured himself. Blowing out the candles, he opened the curtains and sat to watch the moon's outline barely visible against the tufts of gathering cloud.

One more day and it would be over. His war. Intelligence. Freedom. He could not even imagine going home to Luxford and being content.

* * *

Guy Bernard was waiting for her early the next morning as Celeste sidled into the busy marketplace at Les Halles, bread and buns in the basket on her back. If she'd been paying more attention, she could have simply avoided him, but as they'd come nearly face-to-face she had no way of pushing past. The colour in his cheeks was high and there was a certain set to his shoulders that she recognised.

'Are you turned traitor, *ma chérie*?' His greeting dripped with sarcasm. 'After the Dubois fiasco it is being whispered that you are working for the English.'

'That implies I might care more about the outcome than I do, Guy.' She threw this back, this certain truth, for two could play at this game and she knew he had never been in it out of loyalty to France. They were both for hire, to anyone who might pay them well, and this was their strength as well as their weakness. When she saw him relax, her fingers slid away from the blade in her pocket and she breathed out.

She needed to know his intentions, needed to understand just what he might do next and, although it might have been wiser to run, a quieter voice inside ordered patience. Without his connection to the inner sanctums of the agencies, she would have been dead years ago. He had saved her so many times in those first, terrible eighteen months that she could not but be grateful. Napoleon's Paris was not a city easy to exist in alone and a young woman of gentle birth like herself could not have made it through the first week if he had not been there.

She had learnt things. From him. She had learnt to

survive and to flourish. She had risen from the ashes of shame to be reshaped into the flesh of the living, a knife in her hand and hatred in her heart. Guy had taught her how to hone it, how to use it, how to live with the vengeance tempered. She was a thousand different women now in every way that counted. The self that had barely been alive after her father's death was gone. There were too many hurts to want to remember, too many ripped-away pieces that had stopped her being whole.

So when his hand came down across her own she did not pull away. There was good reason in the pretence of it, after all, even for the small time left to them. A front. A necessary deceit. A way to navigate the sticky path of espionage and not be dead.

'You are too alone now, Brigitte. I no longer recognise anything about you, about who you were.'

Once, she had liked Guy Bernard, liked his passion and his energy for a better France, until she saw that there was no morality beneath his desires and until she understood other things as well.

He was dangerous and he drank too much. Before the first year of their marriage was over she had pulled away from the intimacy. They had continued with the charade of it all for another six months for the sake of the jobs they did. Together they were a formidable team and if Guy heard something that she had not, then he made certain she knew of it, and vice versa. The newly invented Mademoiselle Brigitte Guerin was a woman fashioned from smoke and mirrors, after all. Guy had lifted the identity card from a dead whore in the back streets of the Marais because the deceased girl was about the same age as she was and had enough of the same features—hair, eyes, height—to get away with sharing a casual description on the *livret*. Such a paper was enough to allow marriage, to be legal again, to have a history and thus a present and a future; a name change to weave a further ring of protection around the dubious centre of her truth. There was too little trust in Paris to be an outsider for long.

Brigitte Guerin filled the gap nicely and her father's mistakes could not be traced back to it. Guy Bernard's street savvy had afforded her protection and he'd never uttered her birth name again. But politics and the shifting tides of France's fortune had drawn them apart, his anger becoming more and more pronounced and his moods so melancholy she had been able to stand it no longer.

Striking out on her own, she'd taken all the skills that her husband had taught her, skills that crept into her bones even as they made them hollow. He'd followed her for a time, trying to insist he'd change, but she had never allowed him the chance and so he had moved on as well—to other women, some no more than mere girls. She knew deep down that in any other life she'd have barely glanced at him.

'Who are you this morning?' His eyes flickered across her trousers and jacket, taking in the bread she carried. 'The baker boy? The minion of the markets?' He snatched a roll and bit into it, the crumbs falling and catching in his scraggly dark beard. 'Benet wants you to come in and explain what went wrong with the Dubois. He thinks your loyalty is now in question.'

She stood back and tipped her head up at him. 'And yours isn't? Louis Dubois was seven and a half and Madeline Dubois not yet five.'

He swore, using the guttural expletives of the rural west, a hangover from his far-off youth. A mistake, she thought, that would show any halfwit agent who you truly were. Or had once been.

'They were not supposed to have been there.'

'And you think that is an excuse?'

As if realising his slip, he returned to matters of business. 'The English spy, Major Shayborne, is in the city. If you can bring in a prize like that, Benet might trust you again.'

'You speak of the soldier who is Wellesley's master of intelligence?' She liked the sheer amount of surprise she was able to inject into her query.

'Exactly the same. He broke the parole he had given in Bayonne, though in truth he could have escaped any time during the journey across Spain and been back safe in the arms of the Spanish guerrillas. One might wonder why he should do this? Such a question could lend more credence to the story of the Englishman being in the city to take a look around at the military capacity of the Grande Armée. Numbers. Direction of travel. The manner of weaponry and any hint of future plans. When we capture him, he'll be hanged summarily and secretly, that much is certain, for there is too much of the martyr in him to allow anyone the outcry of it otherwise.'

Celeste had found all this out already. Guy Bernard was telling her nothing she did not know, though what he left out was revealing in itself.

They had not discovered the link with James McPherson. They did not know of the American connection either, for she was certain Guy would have mentioned such a thing.

Where was the information coming in from, then? She couldn't ask him. People were on her tail, too; she'd seen them twice today watching from a distance. Strangers. Agents from the Secret Police or the War Office? Or maybe from the Garde Municipal de Paris?

The whirlpool was falling inwards, catching them all with its increasing speed. Facts. Conjectures. Secrets. Napoleon's newest push into Russia had created divisions and it would not be long before everything spun out of control. She should leave Summer Shayborne to his fate, good or bad. He was a man who had taken his chances and come out on top thus far. Luck did not last for ever—she knew that better than anyone. But although her head told her to run from Paris, her feet would not follow.

Foolish sentiment or a prescient warning? Get too close to a case and you could lose perspective. It was the very first learned law of espionage.

Her teeth bit down on her bottom lip in worry and Guy Bernard smiled, misinterpreting the signs. 'Move back in with me, Brigitte. Together we could manage to ward them all off, just as we did before. I can protect you.'

'Oh, I think we are long past such a promise. Besides, who's to say I am not now enjoying my own bene-factors?'

She needed to lead him away from the truth and this was the perfect way in which to do it. Protection money was a tenet he understood and believed in. Sometimes she wondered whether it was all he had left, a shell as empty as her own.

'Benefactors?' He did not sound happy.

'People here pay well for an ear to be listening in the places that count. Bankers. Men with property. If it all falls over, they need to know when to sell, or how to gain by holding on to their assets.'

'And you share your body with these men?' He leaned forward and took her forearm, the back of his hand brushing suggestively against the rise of her breast.

'Whether I do is no longer any of your business, Guy. Cross me and you cross them, too, and they will not be pleased.'

She half expected retribution for such a threat and part of her might have welcomed it. An easy ending. A final peace. She wondered, as she had a thousand other times, where the truth of who she was now lay? Lying was second nature to her, as was subterfuge. Still, she was glad when he let her go.

'The slut in you is not attractive, Brigitte.'

She tensed at such an insult. After her father's death, any morality she had once clung to was gone. Lost in a name change and a marriage and pure plain circum-stance. Indifference had probably been part of it, too. She was so fractured she barely noticed the added ruin of using intimacy to gain information. The bottom of the barrel was not as graceless as she had imagined and knowing she could not fall any further offered a kind of comfort and certainty that felt like a sanctuary.

'Benet wants to see you.'

'Because he thinks I can find this English Major?'

'Wellesley's intelligence officer is a big prize. This for that, so to speak. Reparation. Recompense. Your unquestioned loyalty to France delivered on a plate.'

'With Shayborne as the main course?'

'A better notion than you being served up, I would imagine.'

She smiled.

'And after yesterday's bungle, Brigitte, your friends may also need to find some evidence of their loyalty again.'

She almost spoke, but stopped herself. They would as soon trust a viper in a basket full of eggs.

'I will come when I can.'

He shook his head. 'Benet wants you there in an hour.'

'Very well.'

She wondered if she could bring herself to kill Guy if it came to a head, even as she realised he was probably thinking the exact same thing. He had beaten her a number of times as their liaison was drawing to a close. At first she'd thought she deserved such treatment and had crawled on back for more. When he deliberately broke three of her fingers, she'd left him for good.

Mattieu Benet, the newly crowned controller of the Paris operation, was the first to meet her in the small house off the Rue du Faubourg. He looked tired, his oncoming bald patch crisscrossed with lank strands of dark hair. One of these had fallen from its place and hung on the wrong side of his parting, almost to his shoulders. She resisted the urge to step forward and put it back into place.

He got down to business without mentioning a word of the Dubois. Celeste was relieved, though the fact that he would not question her about her part in it kept her on edge.

'The War Office of Napoleon is keen to find out whether there is any truth in the rumour that Major Summerley Shayborne, Wellesley's chief intelligence officer, is in the city. If the Englishman is here, they are most emphatic that they do not want this to be a problem. They want a short, sharp end to any lingering political complications such a presence might entail.'

'There will be no negotiations for his release, then?' Guy asked and Benet shook his head.

'None. We can take him in for our own interrogation, though, before we dispose of him. The War Ministry is calling for his neck and Henri Clarke has grown more and more bitter with every successful reverse inflicted by Britain. The intelligence sent from the field by Shayborne has been both fastidious in its correctness and highly damaging, and it is time to call a halt on the spy's ability to track what will happen next.'

'Silence him for ever?'

'As quickly as we can. Every office of authority in the city has their men out trawling and a scalp like this is a feather in the cap of any organisation who bags him. I am hoping it will be us.'

A map of Paris was brought forward and laid out, and Celeste saw that a boundary had been drawn around the arrondissement she had visited Shayborne in the night before. They were closing in. Unless he had taken notice of her warning they would catch him, for his circle of sympathetic agents in Paris could be nowhere near as numerous or as dedicated as those he was known to have fostered in Spain and Portugal.

The priests here might help him given their anger against the nationalisation of their churches, but she doubted the ordinary citizen would. Napoleon had been too clever in his promises of better living and raised working conditions. After having been left out of politics for so very long, the proletariat were clinging to the hope of betterment like limpets on a rock in a stormy sea.

Shayborne would be largely alone out there on the dangerous streets of the city, surviving by his wits and his ragtag bundle of allies. She breathed out slowly and turned to speak.

'I have reliable sources here and here.' Her finger touched the map. 'It will not take long to find out if they know anything of the spy.'

'He is still dressed as a soldier, we think. With all the military movements in the city, it would be a clever disguise.'

She frowned as this new jeopardy shimmered and Benet continued on.

'I am guessing he would not be sporting the scarlet

coat of the Eleventh Foot, but likely something more faded and subdued.'

'The uniform of a land with sympathies to France and an axe to grind against the British, perhaps?' Guy spoke and they all mulled this over.

'A good point and a valid one.' Benet signalled a man at a table to come over to join him. 'Lambert. Find out how many of President Madison's envoys are in Paris and what connections they have. It's a highly sensitive area and we will have to be careful, but I want this information on my desk as soon as it comes to hand.'

A matter of hours only, then, Celeste thought. She wondered if any other intelligence services operating in Paris had made the same deductions as had been voiced here. Interrogation meant torture. If they caught Shayborne, he would suffer a nasty end which she would be powerless to prevent. As she chanced a glance at Guy Bernard, she could see a question in his eyes. She looked away.

Sometimes she hated these people with such a ferocity she thought she might simply expire from it. But at other times she felt a hint of an honour that she had long since lost sight of as she worked to protect yet another victim caught in the crossfire of changing politics. This duplicity was both her penance and her salvation.

She saw the funeral carriages as she walked home along the Seine by way of the flower markets and knew the procession to be for the Dubois family. They were leaving the city for Nantes and the rural graveyard where the slain members of the family would be interred.

The image of the dead children made her slow down and lean over, the straps of her empty bread basket falling to one side.

Un malheur ne vient jamais seul. Misfortune never arrives alone.

She thought of her sister, lost to the morbid sore throat by the age of ten, her lone white coffin in the cold family graveyard beside the south-facing wall at Langley. She thought of her mother's madness and her father's grief. Would it be the same here, under the warming summer breeze of France? Was there some other child who had escaped the murders to be worn into sadness by the ripples caused by betrayal, torn in half by regret and circumstance?

Alice. With her golden hair and sweetness. Biddable, pliant and even-tempered.

'It should have been Celeste who was taken. It should have been her.'

She'd heard the words her mother had shouted in the silence of night following Alice's death, heard them above her father's muffled voice of reason. A tightness had formed about her heart that had been with her ever since.

Did she even still have a heart, she ruminated, or was it caught there in her chest among the thorns of fury, tangled in blood and bristles, stone replacing empathy?

Her hand went to her throat and found a pulse, too fast, too shallow and tripping into a battered rhythm.

She would save Shayborne and then leave Paris, reclaiming something of herself in the process because he was a good man, a moral man, a hero, and she had always been the exact opposite.

It was a direction, the first real truth she had had in years.

'*L'enfer est pavé de bonnes intentions.*'

She smiled. She would travel the path to Hell no matter what, but her intentions from now on would only be honourable. She swore it on the departed soul of her sister and on the name of the crucified Jesus.

She felt for the rosary in her pocket, the beads under her fingers providing a physical method of keeping count of the number of Hail Marys she said. She had recited the whole rosary numerous times under the guidance of her most religious parents until Mary Elizabeth Fournier had jumped from her grandmother's rooftop one snowy January morning and fallen a hundred feet to her death. Her father had told Celeste of the unfortunate manner of her mother's death in the evening of the day on which she had lost her virginity to Summerley Shayborne.

'Faith can guide us only so far, Celeste. Eventually it is resilience that keeps us alive. Your mother converted to Catholicism for me, but I am not certain if she truly did believe in it.' He'd had a brandy glass in one hand, an empty bottle in the other, and his eyes were swollen red. 'Perhaps I should never have expected it.'

Resilience.

She swallowed back anger. Her father had missed the point as certainly as had her mother. Sometimes she wondered how little they both must have loved her to have lived life as they did, her mother mired in the troughs and peaks of hysteria or melancholy and her father beset by impossible political aspirations.

She'd been caught between them and had paid a heavy price for it, like a cue ball battered by the solids and stripes into whichever corner might possibly allow a triumph over the other. Well, no one had won the game and least of all her. Her father lay in an unmarked grave on the outskirts of Paris and her mother in unconsecrated ground in Sussex. As far apart in death as they had been in life. She supposed that there at least was some sort of celestial justice in such a fact.

That evening she watched Shayborne's rooms, watched the light at the window and the shadow on the curtains. He was not alone and she wondered who would visit him this late, a puzzlement that was answered a few minutes after as the door opened and a man dressed in the sombre clothes of a priest stepped out.

The Englishman watched him depart, though he did so carefully. It was only the tiniest twitch from the curtains above that gave him away, the candlelight behind blown out now to be replaced by darkness. She wondered if she should follow him, but as the man looked neither remarkable nor familiar she stayed hidden under the protection of a plane tree, the moon filtering little light through leaves on to the street.

Just as she was about to go she saw another figure, his shadow eating up the glow from a lamp above him and with a shock she knew it to be Guy Bernard. He did not hide or melt into the darkness as she did, but stood there like a threat.

An impasse, then, between the three of them. Guy could not know for certain that the English major was anywhere near, otherwise Celeste knew he would have acted brutally and without hesitation.

A suspicion, then. A rumour. The first of all the truths that would come. There were fifty apartments in this block and another hundred in the one opposite. People lived close here and it would protect him. It was why Shayborne had chosen it, she supposed, with its heaving, teeming population and its high percentages of itinerant tenants. Nobody would look twice at a newcomer here for they arrived in Paris all the time, especially those in uniform.

Laying her head back against the dappled trunk, she closed her eyes, her body melting into the shadows inseparable from the tree, and when the first light of dawn rose in the east she saw that she was alone.

Fifteen minutes after the bells of Saint Leu rang out the hour of seven, she followed Shayborne, far behind and away from his sight. She wanted to see who he met and where he went. She wanted to understand his purpose.

She had always shadowed people. It was a big part of her job and she was good at it. No one ever looked back and neither did he. Shayborne strode the city streets as if there was no doubt in his mind that he was safe. He did not act like a man on the run or one who sought the protection of invisibility. He stood so far out that he simply fitted in, a soldier returned from the ghastliness of war and wanting to exist here in the small peace of what was left. He had changed his uniform and she was glad of it, for he wore a dark blue jacket over the grey trousers now.

It was only later Celeste discovered that he had known she was there from the start. He'd left markers and doubled back and then under the canopy of the café, Les Trois Garçons, a hand snaked out and caught at her wrist, dragging her in. Behind striped canvas. Completely out of sight. In a pocket of warm air that held only the two of them.

She did not scream or fight. Her knife was close and her knee was ready, but she'd known it was him from the very first touch.

'Your disguise is hard to fault, Mademoiselle Fournier.'

She smiled because to do anything else would be churlish and small.

'But a bread vendor with the luxury of wasting time is noteworthy and the moon last night was bright.'

'When did you know it was me?'

'A minute after you gave me your warning in my rooms under your wig of whiteness. If you hadn't wanted me to know you, you would not have come.'

She looked at him then directly. In the daylight, his golden eyes were still beautiful, but they were now every bit as distrustful as her own. No longer a boy but a man, hard, hewed by war and suffering.

'There is not much time left for you in Paris, *monsieur*, for your friend the jeweller will have a visit before the morrow's end and it will be much easier for them to find you after that. They already have the arrondissement your apartment is in under surveillance.'

'Do you work for Savary or Clarke?'

'A disappointing question, Major. Try again.'

'You are a lone player trading off the secrets of war to the highest bidders.'

'Warmer.' She did not look away at all.

'Then you play a dangerous game and one that will kill you in the end.'

'And you think I would care?'

There was darkness in his glance. 'Your father might?'

'He is long dead.'

'How?'

'War carries many casualties.' She did not like the waver in her tone so she coughed to hide it. But Shayborne had heard it, she could tell that he had.

'Your father should not have brought you back to France in the first place.'

'No?'

'I told him it was suicide, but he did not listen. Europe was descending into chaos and there was no safe road for any traveller. A simpleton could have worked that out.'

'We are French, Major, and our time in England was at an end. We came home.' The hardness in her words covered over the anger.

'Home to danger and tumult? Home to a rising political anarchy?'

Hell, Shay thought, could the English girl he had known been entirely lost under the cold French woman she'd become? The black scrawny wig of a baker boy shouldn't suit her, but it did and her whole demeanour was more than convincing. Celeste Fournier had always been good at hiding who she was, even as a seventeen-year-old.

'Perhaps such travel was as dangerous as your choice of work, Major? You broke a parole to General Marmont in Bayonne and nobody was pleased. Is the word given by a gentleman such a trifling thing, then?'

'The French were going to hang me.'

'In uniform?' Disbelief lay in her query.

'Not everyone adheres to the rules of warfare. Those soldiers who accompanied me across Spain might not have done the deed themselves, but on the border I was to be handed over to Savary's thugs on Marmont's orders. I had heard it said there were instructions to see that I did not live to cause another problem.' He looked across the street. 'That man over there reading the paper. Do you know him? I have seen him before.'

'At a guess, I would say he is one of the Minister of Police's. I recognise the arrogance and the incompetence. You are right before his eyes and he does not see you because it is me he has in his sights.'

'Why you?'

The sharpness of his observations made her give him the truth. 'A few days ago I tried to help a French family who had strong ties with England and it did not go well at all.'

The crouching danger of Paris at war, Shay thought, and no end in sight. 'So you are under scrutiny for it?'

'Any mistake can be your last here, now that trust has gone.'

'Trust.'

'Everyone says that Napoleon will triumph, but nobody truly believes it any more. By my calculations his empire will be diminishing by the end of next year. I am sure you have heard of his pretensions to capture Moscow.'

He smiled and tipped his head. 'Come to Spain with me, then. We could leave tonight.'

'I'm no longer the Celeste Fournier you once knew, Major, and I'd be safer alone.'

'How can it be safer to be taken to the Military Police and named as a spy?'

'There are worse things than an honourable death in this life.'

'And would it be such an honourable death when they find out you have warned me and allowed me to escape? Such a person could not hope for lenience.'

'And I would not expect it.'

His finger ran across the soft flesh at her throat. 'Your heart is beating too fast to plead indifference, though your father's tutelage in the art of theatre adds a certain truth to your charade. It must fool many.'

'I am not like you, Major Shayborne. My morality is questionable at the best of times and if you believe otherwise you will be disappointed. Meet me tomorrow under the front arch of Les Halles if you want my help to leave the city. At five in the morning. Do not bring luggage. It is your last and final choice. If you aren't there, I shall not see you again. *Bonne chance.*'

Anger sliced through him and he bit down on a reply, but she'd pulled away and was already gone.

Like smoke. There one moment and gone the next. He wondered how she did that, but reasoned the street was suddenly full of pedestrians and she had only been waiting for them to draw near so that she might depart unnoticed. His eyes scanned the road.

Yes, there she was a good hundred yards away, sliding into the alley behind a cart selling fish. His gaze didn't linger, though, because other eyes might well be watching and even a little security was better than nothing.

She'd looked smaller than he remembered and a hell of a lot thinner. And there had been a line of scars circling the sensitive skin above her left wrist. He wondered why.

He had ruffled her calm, she thought, and left her on edge. No one had spoken to her so honestly since her father had died, and the pull to return to England was stronger than she had imagined it might have been.

A safe place. A quiet and beautiful sanctuary. Shaking her head, she turned away into the shadows, causing her to miss the telltale sign of someone hiding.

More than one, she corrected a few seconds later when Guy Bernard and Pierre Alan held her between them, arms splayed across the uneven stone of the wall, the black wig tugged off and thrown down, trampled into the dust.

'Benet has reconsidered your part in the Dubois debacle and has sent us to deliver both a warning and a counsel.' Guy spoke, his voice softly furious, even as his fist slammed into her unprotected stomach, the air viciously expelled from her windpipe, leaving her retching for breath.

'Your other interests are to desist immediately and any further contact with the English shall be taken as treason on your behalf and you will be accorded the appropriate treatment. You are to be made an example of as a message to others, let it be known that there can be no question of loyalty in these difficult times. A tutelage in humility, if you like, and one that reinforces that even the best of us are not immune to answering to the might of France.' Her face was next, the careful punch of a fist bruising her mouth and shaking her front teeth.

For a moment, she saw stars about her, the earth tilting and the warmth of blood running down her chin to drip unheeded on to the rough homespun of her trousers.

'Benet wants to make sure that you realise if there is another incident of such a nature, you will be dead. Do you understand? There will be no further clemency.'

Alan's knife was out now and the slice across the skin on her right hand cut deep into the flesh between her thumb and forefinger.

'Do you understand?' Pierre Alan repeated, menace clearly audible.

'Yes,' she breathed out, feeling the spin of terror. Another few moments of this and she would not make it home, the weakness of shock consuming her former bravado.

'Look at me.' It was Guy's voice now, its personal

intonation alerting her to a new degradation on its way even as his lips came down hard across her own. One hand curled about her throat, holding her there as the other wormed under her shirt and squeezed her left breast.

She saw his intent and the horror of her past resurfaced, moving like wraiths under her skin before the world blackened about the edges and she was falling, her blood slick on the coping stones as her feet went from beneath her.

When she woke she still wore all her clothes and was relieved that he had not followed through on the threat implicit in his assault. Leaning over to one side, she was tidily sick, the contents of her stomach soaking her trousers and running across the bleached stone.

Her nose streamed, her hand smarted and one of her front teeth felt loosened. A lucky escape. A fortunate evasion. The ache in her breast left her dizzy as she fumbled with the buttons on her shirt. He had pinched her there, next to the nipple, pinched her so hard the skin had dimpled and left a red mark.

But nothing was broken. Nothing would be permanent save for the scars inside. Benet knew his business and Guy was a competent servant. If not for her hope of helping Shayborne, she would have been well bent into submission now, too scared to think for herself, let alone act.

They could find her whenever and wherever they wanted and next time she would die. Less cleanly than Benet had directed, she imagined, the rush of lust in

Guy's face unhidden. If he had been there alone without Pierre Alan looking on, she wondered if he could have controlled himself. She was certain he would not have.

A crossroad dressed as a warning. The play of men against a woman. No one knew the true and personal ramifications of what had been threatened, save her.

She sat back and took her hat in her hand, hiding the injuries with it as others hurried past. For this moment she could not walk, fright having frozen her into incapacity. Passers-by would see a drunk perhaps, a youth who could not hold his liquor, a working boy with little sense or intellect and no hope.

Breathe, she instructed herself firmly and began to find air, small gulps at first and then greater ones. The tight alarm in her chest loosened and her teeth let go of the soft flesh inside her mouth.

'Papa,' she whispered when her voice was back, hating the need she could hear in the single word and the tears that stung the cut across one edge of her cheek.

Chapter Two

Shay counted down the seconds following Celeste's departure, wanting to place a good amount of time between them. Safety depended on careful observations and well-planned escape routes.

McPherson would have to be warned, of course. The net was closing in day by day, but he hadn't yet done what he'd hoped to since coming to Paris. He had passed military and political intelligence through McPherson to Wellesley, good intelligence that would inform the strategists and policy makers. But things were coming to a head now and he did not want to miss the last battles of the campaign.

Napoleon and the Grande Armée were Russia-bound and General Wellesley was moving east towards France, chasing the last of the remaining French troops under General Soult out of Spain.

He would quit Paris for the Spanish north. In disguise, he thought, and his heart sank. In all the weeks he'd been in France he had worn his uniform, as he had promised to do. Never before had he broken his promise to stay under the protection of military clothes.

Celeste Fournier was another problem. If she had come to him, then others were probably watching, too, and her vow of help was beguiling. He would like to understand why she had left Sussex so abruptly. He would like to know why she had never made contact with him, why she had slid into the Parisian underworld of subterfuge and sacrifice instead.

A small hole in the canvas allowed him to slip into the backstreet behind the restaurant and up through a series of alleyways that led to Montmartre.

McPherson's apartment was halfway up the hill on the Rue des Abbesses and he was home, setting a substantial diamond in a gold ring.

'The secret police and the War Office have us in sight. You will need to pack up and leave.'

Grey eyebrows shot up. 'Cunningham implied as much when I saw him last. The White Dove warned him.'

'The White Dove?'

'A woman who transfers cachets for us sometimes and one who goes by so many names I have lost the truth of her real one. It is rumoured her father was murdered six years ago by the English.'

'Where was the daughter when this happened?'

'Here in Paris. Another lost soul of the Empire.'

Shay felt unaccountably sick. Was this Celeste he spoke of? Had she been with her father when he had been killed? Had she seen the murder?

'Who does she work for now?'

'Nobody and everybody. I pay her well for things pertinent to the security and success of Britain and her causes. Sometimes she slips in red herrings so even that loyalty is questionable. At heart I imagine she works for one of the clandestine and dangerous underground agencies set up by Napoleon's less salubrious captains. Like everybody else here she needs money to survive.'

My God, such revelations turned all he had once known of Celeste on its head. Spoiled. Impetuous. Arrogant. Brittle and beautiful like her mother, but in a far more spectacular way.

Why would she come to his rooms and risk exposure? Why had she shadowed him? There was something he was missing and he could not quite put it together. The disguises she had sported each time he had seen her made no sense either, for August Fournier had been wealthy and his daughter's gowns the veritable talk of the county. She could have retired into an elegant lifestyle with her looks and her money. She could have married anybody she'd desired and done well. Yet she plainly had not.

McPherson hadn't finished, though, and after a moment he continued speaking. 'The thing is that there is a certain fineness about her that one understands only by degrees. She brought me medicine when I was in bed with a bad chest last winter and only a few days ago she played a role in trying to save the lives of a family caught in the crossfire of politics.'

Now he knew it was Celeste, for she had spoken of the same blunder.

'How?'

'She warned them of the danger. They were about to leave Paris when they were killed.'

'What was their crime?'

'The father had shot a man who threatened his wife, but honour in Paris has many complex layers and most people are entangled in some way or other with government strategy. For all the freedoms Napoleon promises, he keeps a tight rein on divergent thinkers.'

'Which Felix Dubois was?'

'Ah, so you had heard of the fracas? The White Dove has her own thoughts on justice and if I know of her involvement, then others will, too. There were documents found in the Dubois house which heralded British sympathies. Some say they came from her hands. If she is not careful, it will be she who will feel the wrath of suspicion next, if she still lives.'

Shay swallowed and hoped the bread boy had made it to ground safely.

'I have had word that my identity is on the verge of being discovered. Your name has been mentioned as well. Cut your losses now and come home with me to England, James, for Cunningham is already gone. We can leave on the morrow.'

The older man only shook his head. 'To do what? There is no place left for me in Scotland now and I have been here in France for so long it has become my home.'

'A home that is more and more unrecognisable. The causes here are as lost as Napoleon will be in a few short years and your name is certain to be found on the list of those who will be interrogated...'

'If I knew from the start just how it would end, I still would not have changed a thing, Shay.'

'Because you believed in Napoleon's promises?'

'No. The cause I believed in is long since dead. What I want now is justice for all those good souls who perished along the way, those who cry out for vengeance and who believe in equity and truth.'

'The fight is no longer yours, James. It's too dangerous for a start...'

A heavy knocking downstairs had them both standing and they moved towards the back of the room in unison. They had practised for this, expected it for weeks now, ever since Napoleon had abandoned Paris, leaving the political chaos in the city behind him. There were so many factions seeking power in the vacuum of all that was left.

'You first.' Although the older man protested, Shay pushed him through the small opening and lowered the platform with its thick rope gurney. The crash of splintered timber alerted him to the fact that his enemy was close, as did the sound of feet pounding up the creaky staircase.

As he heard the gurney hit the ground with McPherson safely away, Shay knew his own chance of escape had run out so he turned, raising the stool beside him like a shield, a thick twist of rope in the other hand.

They weren't in uniform, a fact that told him the military was not involved. They were also not at all conciliatory. He might have managed something if they had allowed him words, but there were five of them altogether and when the gun fired at close range he felt the bite of it in his right thigh. A coldness spread quickly, his sight blurring. He wondered if the bullet might have hit a major artery or the bone for he could not feel his leg any more. Weakness crawled into his head and his limbs. Then there was nothing.

He came awake in a room and discovered he was bound to a chair. Tightly bound. Two men sat in front of him. One had just thrown a pail of cold water over his head and the shock of it brought him back to consciousness.

'Who are you?'

'Captain John Barton of the American Regiment of Infantry and one of President Madison's envoys.'

'Liar. You are Major Summerley Shayborne of the Eleventh Foot and you have worked for General Wellesley as an intelligence officer in Spain for these past two years.'

'I don't know who you are speaking of.'

'Do you not, Major?'

There was a slight kerfuffle and there materialised before him the face of one of the soldiers who had accompanied him across Spain after his capture by the French Dragoons in the north-west provinces.

'The Englishman's hair is darker now, sir, but his attitude is exactly the same. It is him, I am sure of it.'

'Thank you, Private. That will be all.'

A hard fist glanced across his mouth, tight with fury, the smack of it coinciding with pain. A dislocation of the jaw perhaps. He shook his vision clear.

The second blow jabbed a soft spot in his lower

back and then a third targeted the injured leg. His thigh ached like the dickens. It was a considered torture and a damned effective one.

'Confess who you are, Major Shayborne, and we will leave you alone.'

To hang, he thought, though it did cross his mind a simple knife to the throat might also have been an option. They were in a basement room and the floor was hard-packed earth, a drain of sorts to the side. To sluice away the blood, he supposed, the mess of death easily dealt with.

'Who are…you?' He got the words out with some difficulty.

No one spoke. Not Savary's men, then, for they were braggarts and would have supplied such information readily given the unequal balance of power and the obvious outcome. Not from the War Ministry either. He doubted they would treat a man in uniform like this.

One of the shadowy unit of Napoleon Bonaparte's that James McPherson had spoken of? He'd heard of them, of course, but only in veiled reference, the layers of intelligence deep here and impenetrable. He decided to play them at their own game.

'The Emperor will move the Grand Armée into Russia before the winter. It is his first priority and the vacuum left will allow the English to take back Spain.'

Another slam into his ear, the high squeal of sound inside the drum a direct result.

'Joseph Bonaparte and the Marshals shall be thrown out of Madrid and then piece by piece the victories of Napoleon will dissolve into defeats.'

His mouth was hit this time and he tasted blood. At this rate, he would be dead before they meant him to be. He kept talking.

'Wellesley will chase General Soult back to where he belongs. When the British enter France, no one will stop them for the French military effort lies in disarray. It will be a straight march up to Paris and victory.'

They were getting more and more furious and he knew that Marmont's orders to kill him when he crossed the border all those weeks ago from Spain were still in force here.

He'd given his life's work for England. His death would be for that country, too. It was surprising how calm he felt, how distanced. He wondered if perhaps he were already part way gone to that shadowy place between death and life he'd heard talk of on the battlefields of Europe.

When the door suddenly opened, he was brought sharply back into the moment, the pain skewering through lethargy and dislodging the mucus and blood from his breathing passages. With shock, he saw it was Celeste Fournier who'd walked in, dressed in a harlot's gown, her hair the red of blood, fire and betrayal, and falling in a curling mass down to her waist. There were bruises around her mouth and a bandage encircling the fingers of her right hand.

'Benet told me to come in and identify the prisoner.' Her eyes met his own, but there was no warmth or recognition in them, no compassion for his wounds. Only distrust and fury. They were not blue at all, he suddenly thought, but the pale purple of storm clouds over mountains. The skin on both her cheeks was drawn into hollow pits and her lips were rouged and full and sensual. The colour had bled across her teeth. He looked away.

'You know the English bastard?' The tall bearded man stood now.

'I met him once a long time ago, unfortunately. It is indeed him. I would know him anywhere.'

Her glance raked across him and then down to take in the dark blood marking his trousers at the thigh. Adept at reading people, all Shay could see in her face was disgust, underpinned by a certain distance.

'You are sure? You would swear your life by it, Brigitte?'

She stepped closer and regarded him. 'Marmont wants him dead. Benet wants information. Either way, Shayborne will not leave this room alive. It's up to you how much you make him tell you, Guy. I would probably use the blade. Here.' She gestured lewdly to his crotch. 'Even heroes have their vanities, I should imagine.'

Her head tipped up to the man standing next to her, an overt and shocking sensuality in her expression. The bodice she wore was partly opened and very revealing and she made no effort at all towards modesty. There was something else there, too, a subservience, he might name it, drawn across the edge of lust. She looked like a prostitute about to satisfy a client's needs in the back corner of the harsh streets around Les Halles.

He could smell a perfume on her that was neither expensive nor subtle. Beneath that was the sharp tang of fresh sweat.

'Perhaps I could make him talk, Guy, if you wish to leave me with him for a few moments. Reparation, if you like, for my foolishness.'

Shay heard the laugh of his interrogator and saw his hands slip into the silk bodice of her flimsy dress, large fingers cupping one breast.

'I am pleased to see that you have come to your senses, *ma chérie*. I wish I'd thrashed you more often over the years if this was all it took. You were always a quick learner.'

When he leaned forward to take a pink-tipped nipple in his mouth, Celeste Fournier raised her fingers to his hair as if to gather him in. Then all Shay saw was blood. Even as the dark-haired man began to fall, she had taken the other down, too, with the heavy punch of steel from the butt of her upturned knife. Within five seconds his own bindings were cut.

'Can you stand?'

He nodded, because if he couldn't they were both dead. He had no idea who was outside the room as he'd been brought into it unconscious.

'Follow me, then. We haven't much time.'

She did not open the door she'd come through, but took him deeper into the basement, prising off a vent of some sort and telling him to slip through it.

'Crawl along until you find the second opening on the left. There is a ladder a hundred yards down which goes to the street. Wait for me inside the vestibule of the church Saint Eugenie on Rue de Richer. There is a brown cloak there hanging on the peg nearest the door. Wear it. Do not show yourself to anyone. If I fail to come within twenty minutes, leave the city and travel east. They will expect you to make for the safety of Spain and every road will be watched. Do not visit the jeweller James McPherson. He is already gone.'

'And you. How will you get out?'

She pulled down one strap of her bodice and smiled. 'As easily as I got in.'

He swore even as she showed him a small glass vial strapped to the inside of her leg. Her skin was white like ivory, her thighs smooth and slender. 'If you are caught, it would be wise to fight to the death before they take you. There will be no second chances.'

And with that she replaced the grille so the bars were between them, dividing the light. She used her knife to screw the grate back into place and Shay noted blood seeping through the bandage at her wrist.

Guy Bernard was a threat as well as a bully and Celeste trod lightly past his inert body. She could not be sorry it had come to this, for her debts to him had long since been discharged in full, and more. The other man, one of Guy's younger accomplices, was someone she had never liked, though she was confident she hadn't killed him. When he awoke he would talk, but it was too late any more for caution and she no longer held the taste for brutality.

She rubbed her cheeks hard with her hands and breathed deeply to try to take away the tremors, her tongue coming to the split in her lip. The pulse in her throat beat wildly, but there was nothing she could do about that save summon the strength to cope. If she looked even vaguely guilty, she would never get through the next room alive.

Martin Blanc looked up from his desk and then down again, but not before she'd seen him take in her disarray. With a practised start she fumbled with the silk.

'Interrogation makes Guy imagine every woman wants to bed with him. It is a fault he needs to address, I think, for it is becoming tiresome.'

At that he stood and walked across to her just as she knew he would. Breathing in hard, she sniffed and wiped her eyes with the fabric in her sleeve. She had allowed Blanc small liberties before when she wanted information. This time all she needed was distraction.

'Guy said the English Major is proving difficult and I had no desire to stay and watch his violence. He also said to tell you that it might take a while to gain information and that he does not wish to be disturbed again until he calls.' With a small shake she clutched at the side of the table. 'Perhaps I should go outside and get some air? Could you take me?' Her cloak was on the chair and she shrugged into it, glad for its covering.

Martin Blanc's hand came beneath her elbow as he shepherded her out, past a group of men busy around a map on the table. Out on the street she led him into the doorway of an empty shop, her hands pressing down on the side of his neck with just the right amount of force. Her father had shown her this defence and she had never forgotten the teaching. It would be precious moments before Blanc regained consciousness, though to stop him hurting himself further she pushed him back to sit against the sturdy wood of the door frame and pulled up the collar of his jacket.

'I am sorry,' she said quietly and then she was off, walking fast with her face against the wind.

At the chapel, she found Shayborne stepping out from the shadows, his nose dark with blood, his right eye swelling.

'Come, but hide your face.' She did not touch him or allow him to touch her as they traversed the streets to a part of town she seldom visited. She could not risk the other address and this one was closer anyway. She saw that he limped badly and that his face was pinched with pain under the cloak's hood. Still he followed, doggedly. She was glad of the sudden rain shower to wash away any blood that might have splattered on the road behind him, giving them away.

Inside the apartment, she quickly sought some privacy to dry retch into a hand basin without any sound whatsoever. Killing never got any easier, but her soul had long since been damned.

'The way of life is above for the wise that he may depart from hell beneath.'

Her father had often recited this verse from Proverbs and she believed in its message. She shook her head. There was no hope for her to rise with the angels. The most she could pray for was a quick and final end.

After rubbing herself down with a dry cloth, she looked at herself in the mirror. The blood of Guy Bernard felt as though it had soaked through her very skin, the harsh tang of iron filling her mouth, even as she swallowed. The smear of red lip grease coated the small damp towel she held.

She had always known it would come to this, one way or another.

Spare clothes were neatly folded in a wicker basket and she donned them with haste, stuffing the gown she wore back where the others had lain. A hat, boots and a belt followed. The pistol she slid into a leather pouch and attached her knife beside it, the blade cleaned and readied for the next time. Armed well, just as she liked it.

Rubbing boot polish into her hands and cheeks, she bent to scrape her nails against the rough plaster on the floor. Success lay in the detail and she had been brought up for years on the stories of the demise of the French aristocracy and their unblemished hands as they had marched to the guillotine for a final reckoning.

She felt more confident now, the tremors inside quietened. This was her world and it had been for a long time. There was just one last job to do.

The woman who had disappeared into the room to one side of the passageway was nothing like the dirty lad with the ancient eyes who came out of it.

'Your father lived here?'

'Yes. He rented a house in the centre of Paris when we first arrived back, but this was his secret place, you understand, the hidden part of him that few saw. He wanted it as a place to escape, I think, somewhere he would be most unlikely to run into anyone he knew.'

'Because he was delving into the dangerous politics of a failing Empire?'

'And he was drinking heavily.' These words were said with less certainty. 'The sentence for bitterness and broken dreams. He met my mother here in Paris and then spent years back in Sussex. Perhaps he did not truly fit in any more.'

Looking around, he could see all the signs of August Fournier. The books. The pipe. The furniture in the French style. The violin. As well as half-a-dozen old and dusty bottles of various wines and spirits.

'Did you come here with him?'

She shook her head. 'After he died I kept it on only as a sanctuary to hide in should I ever need it.'

'Because you understood by then the danger of what your father had led you into?'

'In his defence, he truly believed Napoleon would make the world a better place.'

'And has it, for you, I mean?'

Real anger found its way through the careful indifference and Shay was glad for it.

'You know nothing of who I am now, Major, and if you are indeed one of the lucky few whose morals have never been tested, then you are fortunate.'

'You are saying yours were?'

'I am saying that you have to get out of this city before every agent of every intelligence group in Paris tracks you down. I pray what is said of you is a truth.'

His eyebrows raised up. 'What is said of me?'

'You are the wiliest of all of France's enemies and

you can disappear into the very edge of air in the time it takes to draw breath.'

'Flattering but foolish.' When she smiled he looked around. 'Do you have rope here?'

'Yes.'

'And a Bible?'

She went to the shelf and plucked out two tomes. 'Catholic or Anglican?' As he took the Latin Vulgate he saw one of the nails of her left hand had been pulled right off, the bed streaked in blood.

She had never been easy to read, even as a youngster as they had traversed the countryside around Sussex. At sixteen she had let him kiss her. At seventeen she had brought him into the barn at Langley and lain down on the straw to lift her skirts in invitation. She'd worn nothing underneath, save a lacy blue garter about her thigh. The next day she had left with her father to return to France and he was sent to London with a commission to join the army. She would be twenty-five now while he was twenty-six.

Different paths. He wondered if she had thought of him ever.

She was the daughter of a wealthy man who should have been brought out for a London Season. She had no siblings still alive and her mother had been damaged somehow. He could never see that same weak will in Celeste Fournier and he could not now.

'Do you speak the Latin?' His voice was low.

'Yes.'

The past between them slipped back into its place

as he wound the necessities for escape out of nothing. *'Fallaces sunt rerum species.'*

'The appearances of things are deceptive,' she returned, and he smiled. No doubt her father had taught her, for August had been a scholar of some note. 'We'll leave tomorrow, mid-morning. It is the busiest time of the day.'

Gathering all that was needed, he sat on the balcony with his back against the wall, the warmth in the stone from the day gone so he felt the coolness through his shirt. No one could see them. No one overlooked this particular space and the thought crossed his mind that this would be why August Fournier had chosen such a location, hidden as it was from the world. He was glad when Celeste joined him, sitting opposite, her hands clenched around her knees so that every knuckle showed white.

'I shan't journey with you further, Major. They know me here and you will have a better chance of escape alone. For me to rescue you from the hawks and then feed you to the wolves would make no sense.'

He brought the cheroot he'd lit to his mouth and inhaled. It was one of her father's that he'd found in a box on the desk. The red tip of it could be seen in the looming dark so his other hand shielded the glow, just in case.

'Who are you? Now?' He said this quietly, because the violence and sexual innuendo in the basement beneath the streets of Paris was still fresh in his mind, and because when he looked at her across the small distance he could not see one single part of the girl he had known all those years before.

She did not answer.

He tried another question, a distinct catch of distance in his tone. 'You wear a wedding ring. Did you marry?'

'The world is a hard place to be alone, Major.'

'Is he a good man?'

'Once I thought him so.'

'And now?'

She closed her eyes and rested her head against the stone, a pointed refusal to answer imbued in the action. He changed the subject.

'What colour is your hair really? I have seen it white and black and red. I remember it as a golden brown.'

Her good hand crept upwards, pulling down her hat.

'There is much you do not know about me now, Major Shayborne, and the colour of my hair is the very least of it.'

'Once I understood a lot, Mademoiselle Fournier.' He stressed the *mademoiselle*. 'I came the next day to find you and thank you for your generosity in the barn at Langley, but you were gone.'

Celeste felt shame cross her face. 'My virginity was hardly a prize.' There, she had said it, out loud. The words settled into the space between them, a truth many times heavier than the weight he had given such a gift.

But he did not let it go. 'Sometimes I wondered…'

She turned to face him.

'Wondered what, Major?'

'Did you know your father would take you back to France the day after...?'

'The day after I offered you my body? Yes.'

'I thought you had gone because of me.'

His reply made her throat thicken and she swallowed. Now was not the time for confessions with a trail of assassins moments away from pouncing on them. If he was to live, he would have to go on without her.

'Hardly, *monsieur*. There was a whole world of lovers I was yet to meet.'

The double-edged words made her feel sick. She took a deep breath and counted. One, two, three... At twenty she felt better.

He was paler than he had been before and there were bruises on his face from Guy's interrogation. Such wounds should not bring the sweat to his brow, though, and after years of jeopardy she was adept at recognising greater injury. Coming up on her haunches, she shifted across towards him.

'Where are you hurt?'

When he pointed to his thigh, she saw the same dark ooze that she had noticed in the dungeon. Back then she had thought the stain had come from his bleeding nose or broken mouth.

'A blade?'

'No. A bullet.'

'Is it still in there?'

His long fingers felt around his leg and she saw him flinch.

'Probably.'

'Come inside, then, so I can look.'

He hesitated momentarily and then pushed himself up, following her in and unbelting his trousers. The long shirt be wore was patched and patched again. By his own hand, she thought, since the stitching was poorly executed. One thing at least that he was not an expert in. That uncharitable thought had her frowning.

'Here.' He raised his leg, bending it at the knee, and a dark and angry hole on the top of his thigh could be easily seen. Slipping her blade from its leather, she spat on it.

'For luck,' she explained as she saw him looking. 'A gypsy in Calais once told Papa and me that saliva is a way of reducing inflammation and we believed him.' The bullet was an inch under the skin. The metal of it scraped against the steel in her knife and she knew it must pain him greatly.

'It hit your bone and not the pathways of blood. You were lucky in such a deflection, for another inch to the side and you would not still be here.'

She twisted the blade slightly and the bullet came out, a small flattened shell of darkness, and when she observed it she could see it was still whole. Standing, she went back to the basket of clothes and ripped a good length of clean muslin from a petticoat she had stored there.

Her father had always insisted on cleanliness around an injury and the old teachings had never left her. 'Singe your knife in boiling water or naked flame and find a fresh bandage. Do not touch the compromised flesh if you can help it either, for any dirt that gets in increases the risk of death.'

August had got such teachings from books as well as from experience, an academic who was well read and curious. A man who had married the wrong woman and lived to regret it.

Mary Elizabeth Faulkner. Celeste could barely even remember her as being any sort of mother.

She ripped at the fabric with more ferocity than she intended to and rolled the long lengths into one tidy ball. She had not the means to heat the blade. Saliva would have to do.

Shay leaned back against a leather chair as she ministered to him, her hands warm and adept. When she was finished, she knotted the fabric and stood. 'It should have salve to calm the hurt, but I have none here.'

'Thank you.'

His heart tripped over the pain and he bit down on fear. If it festered, he would be dead, for he could not run far on a leg that would fail him. But he said nothing of this to her as he tried to distract himself.

'What manner of a lad are you now?' His gesture encompassed her boy's clothes.

He was pleased when she rose to play his game, the awkward intimacy of tending to his hurts replaced by charade.

'My name is Laurent Roux. I am from the south. My father is ill on our smallholding outside St Etienne du Gres where we grow vegetables for the Wednesday markets at St Remy.'

'And why are you here? In Paris? What brings you to such a bustling city, Monsieur Roux?'

* * *

She wondered at his lilting tone, the music of the high towns of Provence in his words, his accent changing just like that. Multi-lingual and clever with it. A gift, she thought. Was that how he had melded into Spain and found out all the things that would save England? The boy she had known in Sussex was now a vastly different man. Harder. Unknown. Dangerous. The darkness of his hair highlighted the gold in his eyes.

With more care, she gave an extra cover to her pretence, matching his abilities in the cadence of lesser-known dialects. 'I came to learn the leather trade as an apprentice. But the stipend required by my master here is no longer possible and I am called home.'

'The reality of many a lad,' he returned, 'and there is nothing more deceptive than a well-planned application of the truth.'

She smiled then and switched back from the musical Provençal to her more formal Parisian French. 'And how well you play it, Major Shayborne. They hate you here, you know, for your subterfuge. You sit at the top of the list of the public enemies of Napoleon's New France. The secret gatherer. Wellesley's right-hand man. Those are just two of the many names attached to you here.'

His fingers picked at a hole in the leather chair where the stuffing was coming through. 'I am only the shadow of many others. Spain has a dozen factions of organised resistance and all of them are fed by a thousand, thousand watching eyes and ears. The priest. The tavern owner. The woman who sells flowers on the busy streets of a city. The farm boy who passes armies as he takes his milk into the village. A lighthouse keeper who sees ships where they should not be.' His face looked tired as he spoke, the last beams of the dusk fading into the flat grey of night. Such a light hid things, Celeste thought, and was glad of it as she answered.

'Many in Paris believe that the Emperor will sweep away all poverty and disease. Her citizens are certain he will bring a kinder life and a truer way of working and for such hopes they are willing to make any sacrifice required.'

'And you believe this, too?'

She shrugged her shoulders. 'Bonaparte's intentions are difficult to define and he is all the more powerful because of it. A peacemaker who pursues confrontation. In truth, he is not what he once was a few years ago when I would have laid my life down for his dreams and died a martyr.'

'Like your father did by coming back to France?'

'It wasn't quite that simple. Papa had doubts and they grew...' She stopped.

Until they killed him. Until the tentacles of corruption surrounded us both and reeled us in. Like fish on a hook with our mouths wide open.

'Did you harbour the same doubts?'

She shook her head. 'It was always survival for me. I sold secrets for money. I took my skills into the marketplace of greed and I lived.'

'By hiding?' He looked around the room and she saw it through his eyes, meagre and shabby. 'By living in the dark? By never gathering things around you that might make you waver?'

She shook her head more violently than she had meant to. 'The girl you once knew died with my father. I have been Brigitte Guerin for many years, Major. I am not the person I was.'

'Who stays the same, Celeste? Who has that luxury in these times?' His tone was as flat as her own. 'Who taught you to use a knife?'

What, not who, she thought, and stood so that she could breathe more easily and so the hate that ran through her in waves of nausea did not spill out as words she could never take back.

'We should sleep.'

He nodded and turned his face upwards, eyes shut against the moonlight. A strong face with the swell of the battering still around his eyes and mouth. She hoped this would not give him away when he left here, but then she thought if anyone might manage to escape, surely it would be him. She would leave as soon as she was sure he slumbered, slip into the shadows of Paris as she had always done, unencumbered, and disappear.

She wished she could stay, even as she sat there watching him, but there were things he could not know, things she dared not tell him.

Who stays the same in these times?

Once she might have thought goodness would win out over evil, that a just regime could easily shatter a corrupt one. That was only until the blacks and whites had all turned into greys and she had understood the true nature of what was left.

There was no one to help her now. She liked it that way. No recriminations. No honesty. Nothing that would make Major Summerley Shayborne look at her in disgust or pity, because nearly everyone who knew her secret was dead and she wanted to keep it that way.

He was worse by midnight and she knew beyond a doubt that she could not abandon him, his glassy eyes darker when contrasted against the red bloom in his cheeks.

'You need to drink.' His skin felt dry and hot, stretched close across his bones in that particular way of illness. Lighting a candle, she untied his neckcloth and loosened the fabric, an old scar she recognised there. He'd once told her his older brother had pushed him off the roof of a garden shed and he had hit the spikey branch of a lemon tree on the way down. Memories. They were both potent and impossible.

When he sipped wine from a bottle she'd opened, she encouraged him to take more for he needed to drink.

Her mind calculated the possibility of being run down here by Benet and his men. Guy had not known of this apartment and because she had seldom used the address she doubted anyone was watching the place. It might be a hideaway for a day or two, or a week if she were lucky. She pulled the thick velour curtains across the window, but did not dare to light the hearth. It was one of the ways she tracked people down, those hiding in an empty home they thought secure save for the telltale smoke curling into the sky above them. There were lots of secrets to be discovered from the rooftops of Paris and she did not intend her own to be one of them.

'Leave me here,' he said suddenly, the fever dreams

receding for a moment and a small amount of logic returning. 'If they find us...'

'It is safe for a while—'

He interrupted her.

'Who were they? Those who took me?'

'Les Chevaliers. They report directly to the more shadowy members of Napoleon's staff.'

'The knights? And you are a part of that?'

When she did not answer he tried to sit up, holding his head in his hands as he came to his knees.

'The bearded man in the dungeon...?'

'Guy Bernard. He was my husband.'

Shay was breathing fast and she could feel his warmth from where she stood, a good three feet away. She even liked the shock on his face when he was not quick enough to hide it. The sickness, she supposed, since she could not imagine a man like Major Shayborne showing her anything that he did not wish her to see.

'I married him after Papa died because Paris is a dangerous place to be alone.'

'And he kept you safe?'

'For a while.'

'And then...'

'You saw what he was like.'

'Hell.' The word was sharp and angry.

'I made a mistake with the Dubois family and it was a warning.'

'Iniquity in the den of thieves?'

She frowned because he did not mince his words or cover the horror of it with easy excuses. She remembered that about him from before, the honesty and the humour.

'James McPherson said there was a rumour that it was the English who killed your father.'

'He was wrong. Papa ran foul of a faction of Frenchmen who did not wish for the Emperor to rule at all. He was fervent about the hope of victory, you see, so fervent he became careless.'

'And you paid the price for it? McPherson named you as the White Dove. An agent who was kind enough to bring him succour when he was laid low last winter.'

She held up her left hand, the ring on her third finger glinting in the light. 'The myths of war are things that sustain those who might otherwise suffer doubt. Surely you of all people should know the nonsense of that?'

Her words had him turning away. His friend Guillermo Garcia was dead. Lying face down in the grove of the dwarf oaks on the ridge outside Idanha a Nova where they had been caught unawares by French dragoons in the grey drizzle of an early May morning.

It was sheer bad luck that the French patrol had come around the corner just as he and Guille had broken through the cordon. His own insistence on wearing uniform had saved him from instant death, but the partisan clothes of his friend had had the opposite result.

The myths of war that sustain those who might otherwise suffer doubt.

Celeste's words were dragged from the depths of truth. He remembered the dragoon lifting Guillermo's head and cutting his neck open with a single brutal slice.

With only a similar small mistake he'd be in the hands of the French again, facing the very same punishment, and no myths could save him here in the beating heart of the Empire.

'You still wear your wedding ring?'

'It adds protection. Why would I not?'

She looked at him as she said it in a hard and direct way and he thought how seldom she smiled any more.

'I can protect you.' The fever burnt and his thigh throbbed, but he meant what he promised. War had changed her, but it had changed him, too.

'I have no more need of a man's guardianship, Major.'

'No?' He took the hand without the ring and turned it over. Breathing out, he tried the taste of honesty. 'It seems to me as though you do.'

The marks of old scars ringed her wrist, surprising and reddened, the newer slash of a knife still weeping into her makeshift bandage.

She pulled away. 'It is the end of my time here in Paris. In another city I shall be someone else entirely.'

'Your grandmother still leaves a candle burning in your room at Langley Manor, just in case…'

'In case I return,' she snarled. 'To go to court and play the lady as the marriage lines are drawn about me, the richest beau, the wealthiest suitor. I think, my lord, that it is far too late for that.'

'You might play the role of a quiet widow just as well.'

'I doubt that I would be credible, for the many acts

of violence here have rendered me somewhat…spoilt for gentle society.'

'Every soldier who has ever lived faces that battle when they return home.'

'But I am not a soldier, don't you see. I am not in it for King and country. Once I might have said it was for my papa's sake, for family, for justice, for liberty even, but now…I am the dark shadow of war, just as you are its shining light.'

He smiled at such an analogy though he knew he should not have, so intent was she on believing it.

Once, years ago, in the home of a Spanish nobleman he had seen a portrait of a naked Venus lying recumbent on her bed as she gazed at the reflection of herself in a mirror. He remembered the painting vividly because in her face was a conceit he had so very often seen in Celeste's.

The conceited and arrogant Miss Celeste Fournier. Every young swain within a hundred miles had spoken of her beauty then, yet it was he with whom she had chosen to lie. Unmarried, too, though he had offered her the protection of his name after and she had laughed in his face.

And here she was again, denying his guardianship, with a split lip and a swollen eye, a bandaged bloodied hand and scars easily visible at her wrist. No longer conceited, but distant and wary. A broken daughter of her father's unwise dreams.

'Did you ever marry?' Her words punctured the silence.

'Yes.'

Her glance fell down and away, the years between them filled with ghosts.

He wished he might have been able to stand up straight and tell her of it, but his head felt strange and his balance was off so he stayed still and closed his eyes. When he opened them again she was gone.

Chapter Three

Shayborne needed medicine and he needed water. The darkness would allow her some protection as she moved through the emptying streets of a city settling in for the night.

He was married.

The lump in her throat was thick and real, yet she knew any hope for what she had once thought between them was long, long gone. Better to accept it and move on. Better to have never asked him in the first place, too.

Madame Caroline Debussy appeared to be home as Celeste crept through the dark gardens in the opulent area of Petit Champs for the lights were on in the drawing room. This was an address she had come to for refuge across the years and, opening a large door, she let herself in to find the older woman sitting by an unlit fire.

'I have been expecting you, my dear, for there are rumours…'

'Which are all true.' Celeste had not the time to skirt

around the issues and with Madame Debussy she hadn't the inclination to either.

'Guy Bernard is dead?'

'Yes.'

'Then I am glad for it. He was a bully and a cheat and one day he would have killed you. It is said that Benet is furious and names you as a traitor.'

'Which on all accounts I am. But it is not for England I did this. It is more personal.'

'The man you helped escape, the injured English spy?'

'I knew him once…before…'

'*Merde.* Everyone is looking for him. He is an important trophy.'

'Has Benet been here to see you?'

'Not yet.'

'Then I hope for your sake that he will not. But for my father's soul, Caroline, I would ask for two things. I need you to take this money and see that the remaining Dubois children and their mother are spirited safely away from here.' She handed over a heavy silken purse and watched as the woman pocketed it. 'I also need medical supplies.'

Caroline Debussy did not miss a step. 'I will have the family moved south and then on to Italy for we have some contacts there. They will like the warmth and beauty of Rome.' Celeste was glad she asked no more questions. 'The medical supplies are easy.' Bending to ring a bell, she waited until her maid came, instructing the girl to find all the bandages and salves that were in the house and bring them back in a bag.

When the servant left and the door had shut she spoke again. 'If this English major is too ill, you might consider leaving him to fend for himself, for to be hunted hard in the company of such a man in Paris is suicide.'

'I know.'

'There is a cordon around the city and men out looking for you, and when they do not find you they will begin a closer search, door to door. Their orders are to kill you on sight, my dear, without even a word.'

'And Shayborne?'

'He is to be taken alive for more interrogation. If you can get your Englishman to me here unseen, there is a priest hole and perhaps...'

'No. It is too perilous.'

Dark eyes flashed as Caroline pushed herself up. Her lack of height was always surprising. 'I have twists of powders here, Celeste, to be placed upon an open wound.' She unlocked a drawer and carefully selected a few. 'Each one is useful. Start with the darkest and proceed to the lightest.' Her face was lined in worry. 'Your father told me once that you were careless, but I think you are not that at all. I think you have always known exactly what you are doing and if your morals have been compromised in order to survive, then so be it, for mine have, too.'

Celeste looked down on the diminutive woman. Madame Debussy had never been one to coat the truth with something to make it more palatable. 'I shall send you word...'

'Don't, even when you are safely away. If you are

caught, I will know of it. Go to England, to your grandmother.'

Celeste took a deep breath and held it in.

Susan Joyce Faulkner, the matriarch of her mother's family. Stern, strong and opinionated. Disappointed, too, for how often had she seen that curl of anger in her deep blue eyes directed at her, the hapless and fickle granddaughter who was never quite good enough.

When did it stop, Celeste thought, this disappointment in others? Her father had brought her into the chaos of France with barely a backward glance. Perhaps Caroline Debussy did truly wish her well, but even now Celeste looked around and listened, expecting betrayal, understanding that in every word that was said there lay other meanings. Payment. Remittance. Settlement. She could feel the heavy gold coins of it lining her boots and she remembered her father's blood running along the floorboards as he had breathed his last before her eyes.

'If you wait, I will find you the things you have a need of and some food to sustain you on a journey. My brother will be home in half an hour...' Her glance went to the clock.

'By which time I shall be gone.'

Caroline nodded. 'I think it is for the best.'

'Why didn't you marry him, Caroline? My father, I mean.'

'Because he never asked me, my dear, and because he loved your mother before—' She stopped.

'Before she went mad?'

'By then I think she understood the journey your

father was taking her on was for ever. She knew that he would never settle in England and after the death of your sister…'

'She gave up?'

'She tried to kill you and your father both. Twice. I think your grandmother knew of it.'

The shock of the words had Celeste's heart speeding up. She could feel the heavy beat of it in her throat and a memory of being pushed and falling.

'People are all different, my dear. What might break one into pieces may only strengthen another, but August set out his pathway and he followed it.'

'And my grandmother? Did she give him her blessing?'

'No, she did not. She cursed him to hell and back for taking you.'

The lump in her throat thickened at the knowledge of her father's choices. Not so easy, after all.

'After the soldiers came I wrote to your grandmother, anonymously, and told her you were both dead.'

'In a way we are, Caroline.'

Celeste was surprised at Caroline's tears. She had never seen Madame Debussy cry, not through all the times they had struggled side by side, not even when her father lay dying at her feet in this very room.

'It was my fault, all of it. Those who hated your father came here because of me. I was a part of it, don't you see. They had been watching me. They knew what August wanted. They knew one day he would cross a line and that they would have their revenge.'

'A line? What line?'

'Your father assaulted the son of the head of their small faction in a drunken rage because he thought it was the only way to make them stop. By then he was crazy with his hopes for France under Napoleon's stewardship and would allow nothing to get in his way.'

'And I was the person in the middle. The daughter? They could not chance what I might say.'

'You never had a hope, Celeste, not from the moment August set foot in France with his hatred and his zealousness. Mary Elizabeth had wounded his soul somehow and even with my best attempts at loving him I could not bring him back to be the man I'd known as a young girl.'

The penny dropped then. Caroline had watched as they had killed her father here in her house. 'In the end, you did not try to save him.'

She shook her head. 'There is as much danger in caring too much as there is in caring too little. August was a lost cause, but I failed you and that is my greatest regret.'

The moment came rushing back to Celeste, the moment the men had taken her, their arms wound around her own, her dress ripped in anger, the blood of her father on her hands where she had tried to stop the bleeding. Slippery with the redness.

She needed to get away and back to Shayborne. This place was like a spider's web with a hundred sticky threads of deceit mixed strangely with honour—the cutting edge of a politics that demanded the blood of its martyrs. Again and again. Until there was nothing left. Not even grief.

Bundling up the medical supplies the maid had brought, Celeste turned, ignoring Caroline Debussy's quiet plea for forgiveness.

Outside, she brushed away the tears that fell down her cheeks, angry at her emotions as well as at the reminder of the loss she had suffered. She should be used to it, this treachery, but Caroline Debussy was the last link she'd held to her father and now that was gone, too.

When the light of a streetlamp fell full across her she was brought back abruptly to the danger of exposure and stepped into the shadow, her palms splayed against thick and reassuring stone.

She was like a drop of water in a river that rushed to an endless ocean. She was a leaf on a tree in the deepest of forests in some far-off land not yet discovered.

She was alone and she was lonely, the jeopardy of Paris all around her reaching out and searching. Well, they would never find her. Not alive, at least, she promised herself that.

Shayborne was barely conscious when she returned, his skin burning with heat, the wine in a glass beside him untouched.

In the bag, she found the water Caroline had insisted on giving her and was infinitely grateful for it. Soaking one of the new bandages, she brought the fabric to his mouth, glad when he began to suck.

'I thought…you had…gone,' he said finally, his strength returned enough to be able to hold the water bottle himself.

'If I leave, you will die.'

He had the grace to smile and the gesture pulled at her heartstrings. Uncomplicated. Sweet and sad. After the evening with Caroline Debussy, such honesty was a relief.

He saw the flicker of something in her eyes, the choice she had made, he supposed, or the lack of it.

The wound in his thigh throbbed badly and he felt shaky and sick. Once in Spain he'd had the same sort of malady and it had taken him weeks to recover. Here he had a matter of hours before they must move.

Celeste had brought a bag from wherever it was she had ventured and he saw her pull a number of medical items from the canvas. Perhaps it would be enough…?

He winced as she removed the muslin from the wound she'd fastened earlier and winced again as the wine he had not drunk was used to sluice out the open injury. He could smell his sweat and his fear in the small space and knew she would be able to as well. But it could not be helped.

'Does it hurt?'

'No.'

'I like you better when you are honest, Major, and if this does not pain you, you must already be dead. This needs to soak for at least ten minutes.'

'Thank you.' He tried to keep the shaking from his voice. And the pleading. It would not do for her to feel she could not go at all. He needed to leave the choice of it in her hands.

'Once upon a time we were friends. It should mean something?' Her voice held question.

Once upon a time we were lovers, too.

He turned away so she would not see that thought in his eyes.

'Tell me about your wife.'

He had forgotten how direct she could be, how unguarded.

'She was beautiful and kind and sweet. We were married for three years before she took a fever and died within hours.'

'What was her name?'

'Anna.'

He swallowed as he said it because the pain of loss was still raw.

'And you loved her?'

'Yes.'

'Then I am sorry for your bereavement. Do you hold strong religious beliefs?'

'No.'

She brought forth her rosary. 'Would you mind if I recited a prayer for her.'

'A Catholic prayer?'

''Tis the same God. I think our Lord will not mind the difference.'

'Your father was Catholic?'

'In England he had no faith in anything. It was only after coming back to France he decided we needed some extra assistance.'

'Because his political opinions were…extreme, to say the least, as well as foolhardy?'

'There are those here who would tar your actions in Spain with the same brush, Major. A spy is hardly easy company, I should imagine, especially one with the reputation you have garnered.'

At that he laughed, surprising himself with the sound. 'It's all a matter of perspective, I suppose. The French may hate me, but the Spanish do not.'

'But you think Wellesley will win against Soult in Spain?'

'I am sure of it. Already he is on the march towards Santander.'

'And you imagine he might come into France itself?'

'I do.'

'So it will have been for nothing in the end. All these lives lost?'

'I think your father might have said his death was a means to an end. After every tragedy there is reflection and learning. And growth if you know where to look for it.'

'You went to Spain after your wife died?'

'I did.'

'And you thought it did not matter if you were killed because your heart was lost?'

He countered with his own query. 'Is that how you felt after your father died?'

'Papa knew the risks.' Her tone was harsh, the truth leaking out beneath the falsities. 'My father made his bed and everyone he cared for had to lie in it with him.'

'It was uncomfortable?'

'As uncomfortable as anyone else's barbs of conviction can be. He wanted the greater good and forgot about the smaller one. If he'd been satisfied with less...' She did not finish, but grabbed a new bottle of wine, uncorked it and took a generous swig. Then she brought a polished jet rosary from her pocket, her fingers sliding across the beads with both familiarity and grace.

She made the sign of the cross and started on the Apostle's Creed. 'I believe in God, the Father Almighty…' The complexity of religion had helped her recover. A salve. A balm. A way of handing her problems over to a deity who could help shoulder the burden.

Shayborne lay quietly as she recited the Our Father and the Hail Marys, the Glory Be and the First Mystery and when, finally, she had finished, she lay the rosary down beside his leg and found salve and sprigs of garlic in the bag Caroline had given her. There was oregano there, too, and the other more potent powders in twists of paper. She began by using the darkest shade, sprinkling it into the red swollen flesh with care. Celeste knew Madame Debussy well enough to know that she swore by these remedies and that they were highly effective. She said her own private prayer of the Guardian Angel under her breath as she rebandaged the wound and tied the ends of soft linen.

'We will leave tomorrow night. I do not think we can wait longer.'

He nodded, but she could tell all this ministering had cost him much and that he needed to rest.

'If I die—'

She did not let him finish.

'You won't.'

The corners of his mouth came up and then he was

asleep, his hands beneath his face as a pillow as he turned on his side.

She would have liked to have lain down beside him and felt his solid bulk against her own increasingly waiflike state, but instead she crossed the room and found a space at the window seat. The night was neither cold nor warm and she was glad for Shayborne's company here in the silence.

Her papa felt closer than he had for a long time. Once, her mother and father had meant everything to her, until she had seen the truth of them both in the worst of circumstance.

Shayborne had had his share of tragedy, too. Anna. Beautiful. Kind. Sweet. Her last thoughts before slumber were of herself dancing in a London ballroom in the arms of the English Major and laughing as though she really meant it.

The morning brought heavy rain. She could hear it against the glass at the window and feel it in the air.

Shayborne was awake. He was sitting up against the wall, smoking.

She didn't know how long he'd been there—her own slumber had been deep and uninterrupted after the drama of the last few days. She hoped he hadn't been watching her.

'You are feeling better?'

'Much,' he returned, the flash of his teeth white against the gloom of the early dawn. 'This rain will help us, for what man wants to brave such weather, even for the sake of his country. It was the same in Spain; armies hunker down when it pours.'

'Perhaps you give yourself too little credit, Major. It would be considered a triumph for any of the intelligence factions in Paris to bring you in and bad weather won't stop that. The woman I got the medical supplies from yesterday said that if you were caught, their orders were to make certain you were left well enough to be interrogated. Again.'

'And you?'

She shrugged and looked away, feeling as though a ghost had run across her skin, dancing slowly. 'I am as replaceable as the next agent. They will kill me on sight, though I don't plan to make it easy.'

'Then we will have to make certain that they don't recognise us at all.'

'If I come with you.'

'You will.'

She liked his certainty and smiled. To place, even for a small while, the responsibility of her safety into someone else's hands was a liberating—and terrifying—thing.

'Did you tell the person you met last night where you were staying?'

'No.'

'Good. When everyone is scrambling to guard their back it always pays to keep your counsel. Even with friends.'

'You've done that?'

'For years,' he returned. 'The quality of good intelligence is too important to squander on some personal vanity.'

When his eyes met her own, Celeste felt something shift inside her, some primal lurch of desire. Today his irises were a dark amber, soaked in pain, but beneath that lay other emotions, deep and quiet but ready to strike.

He had been hurt like her, she could see that, a hidden sadness that spawned from inside and set the edges of his eyes burning into her own.

He was a different man now from the one she had known.

The innocence they'd both lost made her turn away. It was said that he had that particular ability to read people's faces like books and she did not want him to know anything more of her story.

If she had any sense, she would get up and leave him now. He was stronger than he had been and the fever had waned. Perhaps the inflammation had subsided, too. She did not offer to look at his leg again, because tending to the wounds of a former lover brought up thoughts she had no right to be thinking.

And therein lay all the trouble, a familiarity that was both welcome and dangerous.

It was dangerous to cross a line again that she had still barely recovered from the last time. Through all the years of not seeing him, she had nevertheless kept a firm grip on his movements and successes. He had been so very heroic, his bravery spoken of from one edge of Europe to the other.

Wellesley's magical master of intelligence who could escape from any trap set for him, the wily cleverness and the ability to camouflage himself leading even the most jaded of partisans to offer him help as he passed between armies and through towns and cities ransacked by his enemies.

An unrivalled chameleon. It would be wise to tread carefully around a man who was this sort of legend.

Leaning forward, she dragged out a small pistol from her bag. She had two of them and knew that whatever weapons he must have carried before meeting Guy Bernard would be long disposed of.

'This is for you. It's loaded and there are more bullets and dry powder in the double-leather pouch.'

He looked at what she was offering him, but did not reach out. 'I seldom carry a weapon. But thank you, anyway.'

The shocking truth of what he had just admitted sunk in. He would use his wits instead of a bullet.

'Another difference between us, then, Major?'

He frowned.

'A stranger's blood on one's hands has a stench to it. It is a dividing line. Even the most slow-witted might know it as such.'

He took her fingers into his own at the words, uncurling the anger and tracing the marks on her palm. Such a touch kept her silent, the heat of him burning into desire.

'Then write a kinder story across what has been, Celeste,' he said finally.

'Fairy tales have that certain ring of untruth to them. A sleeping beauty. A poisoned apple. An unstable mama who loved one daughter a lot more than she did the other.'

The words came from the pit of her stomach, unexpected, furious, desolate. She'd never disclosed such a grief to anyone before.

'Then that was Mary Elizabeth's problem and not yours. Taken to its full conclusion, your philosophy would expound that I should be held responsible for the death of my own mother. She caught the same sickness I had just recovered from and it killed her.'

She had forgotten the sorrowful story of the Shaybornes. Two young children left motherless after the Viscountess had been taken by fever.

For a moment, reason usurped guilt and the anger in her heart lightened. He had been good at words, even back then. It was what had drawn her to him in the first place, this wisdom, for in the Fournier family there had been a decided dearth of it.

She stiffened at the thought here in the dawn light, only one step ahead of the clutches of peril. The sun had not even risen fully yet, but the day felt hot and worrying, a dozen agencies on their tails and nowhere safe to run.

If he dies, then the last piece that is good in me will go, too.

His eyes were of gold edged in bronze. She wondered what Anna had seen in them when she had stood before him, the kind, sweet wife of a thousand days.

Love, assuredly, and strength. Bravery, too, and cleverness. Such perfection worried her.

If he was not so sick, she might have kissed him full on the mouth, just to see if there were other things in him that were baser, less fine, but a shout from below had her tensing.

Shayborne tilted his head to listen. 'It's a drunk, a soldier who wants to forget what has been and live only for this moment.'

'You can hear that in his voice?'

He looked up. 'The sky is lightening on the Sabbath and he is far from home. There is a loneliness that is easily felt.'

'Have you? Felt it, I mean?'

He shifted his position and she saw the truth in his face. 'Many a time and in many a place.'

'How did you begin, then? What led you to become a spy?'

'A few years ago I brought corn, sheep and cattle through the French lines in Portugal to Wellesley's troops. The arrival of transports bringing rations had been delayed, you see, and there was a serious supply problem of food around Torres Vedras.'

'You led live animals back through the ranks of a starving enemy?' She could not believe his explanation.

'Well, the French fear of the guerrilla bands helped me. Napoleon's troops were reluctant to venture into the darkness looking for trouble if they heard noises in the night and so there were wide, unpatrolled gaps.'

'Which you found?'

He laughed. 'I'd already reconnoitred routes and arranged passwords.'

'Not all luck, then?'

He ignored that and carried on. 'The whole enterprise was remarkably successful and gained me the confidence of General Wellesley. After that I found further employment in watching for the movements of the enemy and reporting back.'

'Still in your uniform? It's what we had heard here in Paris. That you danced through the lines of Frenchmen in your scarlet red.'

'I was a professional soldier who wore a wide and sombre cloak.'

'Because in disguise you would have been summarily hanged? Like John André was in the Americas when he was discovered out of his uniform and stranded.'

'That, too,' he said quietly and reached for the bottle of wine beside him.

He remembered this. This sort of conversation. Her wide knowledge of historical events. It had been the same all those years before as they had sat outdoors in Sussex and talked for hours. She never faltered or became boring. She kept him on his toes both then and now. Even with Anna he had not felt this shock of connection.

The thought made him swallow hard. His wife had been kind and sweet, but she had not been…exciting. Hell, that was an even worse thought than the previous one, the betrayal of a woman he had loved crawling under his skin.

Celeste's hair stuck out from under the cap, cropped unattractively. She had probably cut it herself as the back was longer and less mauled. Her eyes were smoky, distrust written across them. But even after years of fear and danger she was still beautiful. So beautiful he turned away.

'You'll have to bulk up your shoulders if you are to be believable as a lad.'

The change in topic had her standing, a full frown on her brow. 'I don't need tutelage from you in how to be convincing, Major Shayborne. I have existed as a variety of "lads" without problem in Paris for years.'

'Without problem?' When he stood he put pressure lightly on his wounded leg and was glad when it held. 'You are known as the White Dove in the circles of espionage. A woman of mystery, McPherson says. A woman who has served many masters.'

'Mystery is one of those imprecise words that holds a lot of different meanings.'

'Why did you risk everything to save me?'

'I was dead even before I warned you, Major, and it seemed pointless to die for nothing. So I thought to make it count.'

'Count?'

'You are a saviour to the world who despises Napoleon and his ruthless tactics. There are many here who hold no sway to vent their voice for dissent and yet by your actions you gave them hope.'

'People like you?'

She watched the words form on his lips and saw the truth of them.

'My father believed so strongly in Napoleon's ideas that he died for them, six years ago in the house of the woman I met last night. Madame Caroline Debussy. Perhaps you have heard of her?'

'The daughter of the Mayor of Léon?'

'You are well informed, Major, but then of course you would be. Papa was murdered after she betrayed him. She told me that herself yesterday.'

'A hard truth.'

'And there are so very many more of them.' Her hand came forward by its own accord to stroke down the line of his cheek. 'I never forgot you. At least know that.'

The flint in his eyes made her swallow for she wanted him to feel as she did, even if nothing at all could be done about it. She wanted such a power between them, pulling them back to a time that was more innocent, a time when she was still in control of her own fate.

She felt the heat of him rise against her skin, saw the heavy beat of his heart in his throat and heard the shallowness of breath. And just for a moment, in the new dawn of a breaking day, Celeste felt less broken in the intimacy of his company. Then he moved, the anger in him palpable.

'If they identify me on the road, you are to leave without a word.' This order fell into the space between them, unpolished and harsh.

Clasping her fingers behind her back, Celeste wished she might have been braver. It was easy to play the siren when the mark was a man who meant nothing at all to you. But with Summer Shayborne such a charade would not have been a lie.

He did not want her and she was too afraid to demand to know why not.

'You are a slut, Brigitte. You use men to gain only what you want.'

Guy Bernard's words came back to her, whispered in hate.

'Your father told me once that you were careless, but I think you are not that at all. I think you have always known exactly what you were doing.'

Caroline Debussy's summary of her character was closer to the truth. She *had* known, for behind the slaughter of her morals there lay an attempt to protect herself against the nothingness that crouched inside, the ennui that made her sell herself cheaply and without any care whatsoever. The dissolution of responsibility, she supposed, the final acceptance of chaos.

She was her mother's daughter in more ways than she knew, after all—shattered inside, irreparably broken. Too scared to jump, too ruined to settle. The props of a husband and a social position that had kept Mary Elizabeth going were missing in her own existence and yet she could not quite give up. Not when this one last chance had been provided so unexpectedly.

'The freedom of lust is a balm for any emptiness, Major, I promise it.'

The tick at the side of his jaw was the only movement in a face set in cast stone.

Why had she touched him like that and showed herself so blindly when until now she had only lived in lies? He did not even want such honesty; she could see he did not in the stiffened lines of his body and in the quick sorrow across his face.

Pity.

The one emotion she hated more than any other.

Chapter Four

Had Celeste just propositioned him with her body? Did
the weight of lust and a quick tumble mean nothing at all
to her save for a momentary relief of an all-consuming
emptiness? He took a deep drink of red wine. Perhaps
he had misheard things in his sickness and read her
wrongly in a way he seldom did with people? Usually
he was so much more certain than he felt now. Resolv-
ing not to make more of it with an answer, he turned
and searched through the shelves nearby which were
full of artefacts.

'Is there a razor here? An old one of your father's?'
August Fournier had been a man who had always presented himself impeccably.

Nodding, she pointed to the room he had seen her
come out of when they'd first arrived here. It was a bath
chamber and there was a large wicker basket containing
an oddment of clothes next to a basin. Looking at himself in the mirror, Shay felt strangely disconnected and
scattered, a bloom of red on both cheeks and his eyes

bright with fever. He wondered about the properties in the medicines of Caroline Debussy, for his wound and the ache in his leg felt lighter, less distinct.

The harlot's dress Celeste had been wearing in the torture room of Les Chevaliers lay across the top of the basket. Rummaging through, he found other things that August must have once worn and kept as disguises. He was pleased to see the brown habit of a monk among them.

The razor was old, but it would be sharp enough to do the trick. He wished his hands did not shake from the fever, but he steadied his left elbow against a shelf beneath the mirror and set to work. The corked bottle filled with water nearby was just what he needed.

Ten minutes later he smiled at his reflection. The Pyrenees lay to the south through hundreds of miles of French soil. He could follow the river which would lead him into the hills. The French presence would be less obvious there, caught as they were protecting their interests in northern Spain and Portugal.

And if Celeste Fournier elected to come with him, even with all her nonsense on the freedoms of lust, he would be pleased.

For so very long he had been sad. But since meeting her here in Paris, his melancholy had been lessened and despite such jeopardy there was a new tingling of excitement. The promise of something he could give no name to. He prayed to God that they might escape from the city into freedom and safety.

The knock on the door had him turning as it opened.

'I thought perhaps you might be…' She stepped in, her eyes widening at the baldness of his pate.

'You thought I might be using the razor on my throat instead of my scalp?'

A dance of lightness in blue eyes was the only reply.

'No matter what happens to me here in France, I would fight for my life, Celeste. I hope you would do the same.'

Her mother's demise came to mind and he could see she had been thinking along the same lines. He cursed Mary Elizabeth Faulkner Fournier anew.

'Perhaps when you are ready to leave I will come with you, Major, for it is raining harder than I have heard it do so in a long while and that might make it safer. I can't bring the medicines, though, for if we are searched…'

'I'll change the bandage before we depart and leave it at that. The cheese and bread can come, but leave the pistols behind. Bring your blade only.'

'I am not sure if I could pass any close inspection, Major.'

'Then let us pray it will not come to that.'

His voice was changing even as he spoke into the pious, humble cadence of a servant of the Lord. With his closely shaved head, she could now see the light colour of his hair was back. In the sun it would show blond and the tips of his eyelashes were almost a white-gold.

'Is there a safe box here? Something no one else would find easily if they were to search the place?'

'Under the hearth,' she replied and led him over to the fireplace. A quick catch of stone and a space opened, a space large enough even for a small person.

'Papa had it fashioned for me.'

'Did you ever use it?'

'No.'

God, everything she ever told him of her life communicated other things to him as well. He cursed August and Mary Elizabeth Fournier for their careless guardianship of a daughter who should have been safer.

'Put the pistols in here along with your harlot's dress and the white wig.' He had gathered up the strands of dark hair that he had shorn off himself and placed them in a twist of paper. These would go in there, too.

'Let them guess who we are now.' He jammed the medicines in the hole as well, keeping two twists of paper which he stuffed into the bag. The old marked bandage that had been around his thigh was also carefully hidden. Weakness was something he wanted to keep concealed. One sniff of weakness and the dogs of war would be after him with even more tenacity.

Finding a sheet of paper and a quill pen, he laid it on the writing desk.

'Make up a fictitious name and address. Tell the recipient that you will be leaving for the north coast and that you will be there in two weeks if all goes well. Sign it with the name you are known as here and put as high a note as you can afford inside. I'd give you some, but they took everything in my pockets. The money should distract them. When you finish, date it and hide it in the bookshelf. They will find it.'

He was now circling the room, seeing it from the point of view of an enemy. Emptying the last of the wine into a glass, he wrapped the vessel in fabric along with the cork. Bundling this up he placed it into the bottom of the canvas bag that Caroline Debussy had bequeathed her. He took one of the small silver plates from the mantel and shoved it in, too, before picking a miniature framed portrait off from the wall.

August's great-grandmother. The woman was dour and frowning, her clothes as dark and sombre as her mood.

'She will do as the blessed Saint Barbara, one of the patron saints of soldiers,' he said suddenly. 'A protector.'

'For you?' Celeste could not quite understand what he meant and he shook his head.

'A sop for all those who will chase us. Offer them up a prayer of guardianship and they will forget their suspicions of us.'

'You know of such a prayer?'

He raised one hand and touched her on the head, speaking in low tones.

'He that dwelleth in the secret place of the most High shall abide under the shadow of the Almighty. I will say of the Lord, He is my refuge and my fortress: my God; in him will I trust...'

She looked at him in amazement.

'Psalm Ninety-One,' he continued. 'The soldier's verse. God gives four instructions to quell the sense of fear that rises in the hearts of those who fight.'

Celeste was astonished at his competency. How did he do it? What sort of a mind could keep in its grasp the prayer of aiding those who fought for their country when he had professed himself a disbeliever who did not follow any religion? Even she as a practising Catholic had no rote memory of such an entreaty.

'Part of my job in Spain was to reassure those around me that what would happen next was hopeful. The first instruction, "you will not be afraid", was crucial because after that the others would fall into place.'

'The others?'

'You will trust, watch, move forward and pray.'

'And you did that?'

'I never prayed much. Perhaps that was why they caught me finally, though one of the last human freedoms is to choose how you might react to new and unwanted circumstance.'

'And you chose to fight?'

In his eyes the humour doused and Celeste was certain there was another story there. With care, she brought her rosary from her pocket. 'I think you should have this, then. It would be an expected accoutrement of someone so very devout.'

'It was August's?'

'Yes.'

'I will give it back to you as soon as this character of a priest is no longer needed.'

She saw him draw the beads through his fingers and place the rosary in one of the pockets in his oversized habit as she nodded, the heavy silver crucifix hanging around his neck bright against brown cloth.

'If I die, take it to my grandmother. She thinks I am dead already, but...'

'You'd want her to know the truth?'

'Yes.' The word came from some place deep inside, a connection that was not as broken as she had always imagined it to be.

Summer had turned away already, collecting two blankets from the leather sofa and stuffing them into the bag with a ball of rope he had found.

'I'd like to take more of use along with us, but a Catholic priest would likely have little in the way of earthly possessions.'

Her own persona was forming, too, as she gathered another sharp knife, a set of chisels and a mallet from her father's workroom. August had taken up working with leather as a way of relaxing and she often watched him at it. Another strength, she thought, and added a punch for any holes needed.

If anyone asked her about her work as a leatherwork apprentice, she could answer with some expertise. It was the best she could hope for because, if not, she would place Summer in danger as well. The weft and warp of circumstance had strange ways of tying one back into the fabric of life.

They left just after ten o'clock in the morning, the rain having eased, although the wind was high. The marketplace at Boulevard de Clichy was busy, the vendors well into selling their day's wares.

There were soldiers on the far side of Place Blanche and by the slight turn of head Celeste knew that Summer had seen them, too.

The trick was not to falter or hesitate. That was what

the hunters would be looking for, that momentary stoppage or the first change of direction that would be the pointer to complicity. She had done this herself, looked through a crowd for the very same small thing over the years. So she kept her chin firm and walked behind Shayborne. He went slowly, the slight limp less noticeable as he spoke to a man next to him in a jovial way, of the weather and travel and the price of bread. Not just the two of them now, but others, she thought, a family to draw them in.

'You are a priest who hails from the south, Father?' Celeste was close enough to hear the conversation between Summer and the man next to him now.

'Indeed, I am. I have had word that my mother is ill and so...' He stopped and she could hear the grief in his words.

'Then you must let me send you on your way with some bread and cheese. Maria?' A woman she had not seen joined the man along with three very young children. 'Could you give a wedge of cheese to the priest here?'

The soldiers were to their right now and close, but without any hesitation whatsoever Summerley Shayborne stopped to take the offered fare.

The soldiers gestured them on, a family who were travelling together, their gazes lingering on others now, smaller groups, people who loitered alone. And then they were in the wider alleys of Place Clichy, disgorged into space. A tavern full of patrons lay before them and, after offering his farewell to the family group, it was to this that Shayborne led her.

Taking a small seat to one side of the room, she squeezed in beside him as the barmaid came over with two tankards of ale.

'The fellow over there sends you these with his regards. He hopes he might join you?'

'I would be honoured,' Shayborne replied and lifted his glass to a tall man in the corner who ambled over and sat down, too.

'It's not a good day out, Father. Is it a room you'd be wanting?'

'A meal might be more to our liking.' Summer pulled forth a purse that was thin and light, placing it down on to the seat beside him.

The man was quick, Celeste had to give him that. Before she could blink an eye his hand had slid across the wood and replaced it with another purse almost the same, only this one was far heavier. When Summer lifted it again he gave no sign at all of anything being different as he extracted a few of the coins.

Summerley Shayborne knew this man and he had expected him to be here at this time on this day. As she helped herself to some of the food his eyes caught her own. *Trust me*, they seemed to say, and her fingers slid back from the knife at her belt.

'My sister and her husband own a place a few streets west from here. I should imagine they will be pleased to put you up for a few nights for a reasonable price. Do you know Boulevard Malesherbes?'

'Indeed, I do.'

'Here is the address, then.' He pulled paper from the bag at his belt and proceeded to write out his direction, though as the clock on the wall behind them boomed out the hour the man stood. 'I will leave you to your meal. *Bon appetit.*'

Then he was gone, out into the street as the noise in the tavern rolled around them again, convivial and loud. She did not speak, though, as she processed the events of the past few moments in silence. The bread was fresh and the beef stew tasty. As she ate she realised it had been two days since she'd had a proper meal of any sorts and she was starving. Shayborne ate, too, his face set into a smile, though the tight white of his knuckles told her that danger was close somewhere. Breathing out, she copied him, relaxing the lines of her shoulders against the wall behind and tipping down her hat.

The two men knew each other, that much at least was plain. How had he set up this meeting before he'd ever had the need to? The barmaid watched them from her place across the room. A new student in the game of intelligence, Celeste supposed, for she herself would not have glanced across once.

Sometimes she felt ancient.

'We'll leave Paris tomorrow.' He said this quietly, the tankard hiding his lips.

When she nodded he turned away as if his words explained everything. And perhaps they did. Even in a foreign city, Shayborne had set up contacts that were in place should he have a need of them. There was a sort of artistry in such forethought, as well as comfort. After six years of existing in the underbelly of Parisian espionage she had not managed to weave a safety net around herself at all and such negligence said as much about her as it did about him.

He was a man who did not operate alone. He trusted others and depended on their integrity, something she had never grasped the knack of. His contacts were solid.

She'd always paid others well, even for questionable loyalty, whilst he garnered his respect merely by being the sort of man that he was. Honourable. Swallowing, she was saddened by the comparisons between them and, when the meat stuck in her throat, she coughed and took a deep sip of the ale.

Perhaps it had been a mistake to accompany him, after all. Perhaps she should have disappeared after saving him in the dungeon of Les Chevaliers when he still thought her…worthy. Such a word made her smile because in truth she was so far from being anything like him.

'You are enjoying the meal?'

For the first time since their arrival at the tavern she looked straight at Summerley Shayborne. 'It is always enlightening to see a master at work.'

'Hardly that.' The light caught at the new growth on his chin.

'I have seen your friend before. I cannot quite remember where.'

'I wondered if you might have. He recognised you.'

'Is he…safe?' The last word was whispered though the noise in the room was substantial.

'We'll talk of it later. Right now we need to go.'

She saw him glance at the clock in the corner. Half an hour exactly since the man had departed. Further instructions had been given unsaid. He left a silver coin on the table.

Outside the sun was shining through the rain in that particular way of summer deluges. The small drops of it marked his habit in a darker colour. Celeste liked the coolness on her face.

Five streets to the south-west they came to the Boulevard Malesherbes. The man from the tavern was waiting in the vestibule and beckoned them forward. Three more flights of steps and they were in front of a door that was green, the paint peeling so that a brighter yellow showed through.

Inside, the place was tidy and well furnished.

'I've been waiting for you since the day before yesterday, Shay, for Axel said you had been taken in by Benet and Les Chevaliers for questioning.' His eyes came across to Celeste, looking her up and down.

'Brigitte Guerin.' Summer gave this introduction, the protection of the name telling her a lot. 'She got me out.'

'Perhaps only to sell you off to someone else at a higher price?'

Celeste tried to school her annoyance.

'Brigitte, meet Aurelian de la Tomber.'

Now memory clicked. 'I know of you. You are one of Clarke's men and your family owns the most expensive house in Faubourg Saint Honoré. Aristocrats who have survived the reign of Terror virtually intact?'

'Impressive.' De la Tomber smiled and she thought then that he was almost as beautiful as Shayborne. She had never met him directly, but she had heard of him. A dangerous man by all accounts, a man who played a game a thousand times more convoluted than her own. Right now he only looked puzzled.

'You'd be best to stay here for a day or two until the heat dies down. I shan't come back again until tomorrow morning for it'll be safer that way. There is food and water in the kitchen and good wine, too. My agency thinks you have already left Paris, but there are others who are not so sure. They know you are wounded. A bullet to the thigh by all accounts and not an easy thing to walk upon?'

'It is better now. The merest scratch.'

'I have doubts that the minions of Benet are slipping so badly in their expertise of torture.' He looked at the habit and at Shayborne's shaved head. 'The persona of a devout Catholic priest has a certain power in it. I hope you know your verses.'

'Napoleon has his detractors in the church, Lian, and there are very many places in which to gain sanctuary and have few questions asked.'

'Wellesley is offering a substantial reward to anyone who can extract you from the French. He hopes you might simply turn up to claim it yourself if you can make it to the border of Spain...'

Shayborne stopped him. 'I have not yet decided which route we will travel.'

'You will stay together, then?' There was a heavy frown across his brow, but he did not pursue such an insult further. 'There is more money in the desk and weaponry in the space behind the painting of boats in the hall. If you have need of me, leave a candle in the front window at eight o'clock in the evening and I will come.'

'Thank you.'

'Oh, there is one more thing. Madame Debussy said that if I saw you, I was to give you this, Mademoiselle Guerin.' He turned and lifted a book from the table, handing it to Summer.

So de la Tomber knew of her relationship with Caroline. That fact had her heart racing.

It was her father's journal. Celeste knew the cover like the back of her hand and it was all she could do not to move forward and snatch it, her teeth digging into the soft flesh at the side of her mouth to prevent herself from speaking.

When he had gone, Shayborne passed the book over and she slipped it inside her jacket, every fibre in her body aching to open it. Not now. She needed time and space to read what her papa had written. At this moment it was enough that it was there, next to her heart. Safe.

Aurelian did not trust Celeste and Shay wondered what their connection was for the book meant something, too. He could see the pulse in the soft folds of her throat beating at a pace almost twice what it had been before. So many possibilities. He seldom left things to such chance and felt uneasy because of it.

Part of him wanted to flee from Paris now, before the darkness came. If he had been alone, he would have, but Celeste Fournier looked tired, the rings beneath her eyes almost purple in this light. There was grazing on her chin, too, and a cut on the bridge of her nose. The brutal cold-hearted woman who had come into the dungeon of Les Chevaliers and saved him had disappeared completely.

Instead she looked lost and uncertain. And damn young. The smoky bruised blue of her eyes held a thousand thoughts, each one turning through worry before she could hide it.

Had she been anyone else he might have held out his hand in comfort, but too many emotions shimmered between them and he was cautious.

'You need to sleep. I will take the first watch.'

Outside, the day was darkening, more summer rain on the horizon. He was glad she made no answer, but moved away to find the bedroom. Her footfalls were soft and his fingers uncurled from their tight fists as he heard that she was gone.

'God, help me,' he prayed under his breath, frowning as he realised that it was the absolution of lust that he asked for. He remembered her scarlet lips and the pink-tipped nipple before the man she had used her knife on had closed his mouth about her breast.

The freedom of lust is a balm for any emptiness, Major, I promise it.

It had been almost three years since he had lain with a woman and Celeste Fournier's easy offer had set fire to a libido long asleep. It would mean nothing to her, he knew it, a quick toss of passion and a quest for completion, for she had told him so exactly.

Hardly, monsieur. *There was a whole world of lovers I was yet to meet.*

The anger in him smothered desire. Lian de la Tomber

hadn't liked her. He had seen this in the eyes of his friend.

Celeste thought she had killed the bearded man torturing him in the dungeon, but he did not think she had. He'd seen the twitch of his fingers as they had left the room and the shallow pulse of life still at his throat.

Guy Bernard. Her husband, a brute and a bully. He had seen that himself first-hand, for when she had allowed the thin silk of her bodice to fall away from her shoulders into bareness, he'd noticed other bruises there. Marks of passion or of violence?

She was thin but rounded and the sensuality that he'd seen in her as a girl had only multiplied in womanhood. He shook his head and banished such a line of thought, glad for the shapeless habit that would not show any sign of his body's response.

She went to him in the darkest hours of early morning because she heard him call out in some nightmare of the soul.

Pulling back the bed coverings, she slipped in beside him, wearing only her thin camisole. Light. Amorphous. Barely there. She was hot and wanting, her breath sliding across his face as her hands crept lower.

She felt him thick and warm and ready, his dreams translated into engorged flesh and heat as she positioned herself across him. When his eyes opened into wakefulness she saw shock, passion and anger before resistance fled.

Hers.

He was hers in the blink of an eye, filling her, deeper

and tighter, the emptiness beaten back, all her shadows in the corner.

She did not want it to be gentle. She did not want a quiet, peaceful joining. She wanted the pain of lust driving them both, squeezing out memory, breathless with feeling. She sucked at the skin on his neck and knew she would mark him, bruise him. Her nails, short as they were, left gouges as she urged him on.

It was the only time she could ever lose herself, the only time she forgot all that was as she reached for rapture, until he turned and rose across her, pumping in, finding her centre in a hard and relentless power.

The muscles on his forearms were veined, his corded throat straining for his own release as hers suddenly beached upon them, wild and strong. She cried out and he covered the sound with his mouth, teeth at her lips as he finished himself.

Like a death.

Certain and for ever, the heart stopping before it made its way back into life.

Unwillingly.

Always the same.

She swiped away tears and got up, leaving him there in the night with the evidence of his desire running down the soft skin of her inner thighs, the smell of sex and oblivion on the air.

Celeste had exited the bed with as much haste as possible, leaving him lying there with his heart pounding and his breath hoarse and ragged.

'Hell.' The word slipped from him in a quiet liturgy of disbelief. What happens now, he thought, after this?

He could hear her dressing in the other room, replacing the armour that she had shed in his bed. He'd woken from a dream with her there above him and both worlds of desire had collided into the reality of their joining.

As it was meant to be, a small voice echoed inside him. As he had never felt it before, another voice added, and he turned on his side to look out into the night. Pure lust. Only the physical. He felt the driving force of his want still there, crouched in every fibre of his being. Her scent was there, too. Musky. Undeniable.

His discarded habit and her rosary lay on the chair beside him. A fallen servant of the Lord, lost in the thrall of the flesh. Even the bullet wound in his thigh had ceased to ache momentarily.

Was it only this once that Celeste meant to bed him? She had not uttered a word. That worried him. Sitting up, he leaned against the wall and pushed the sheet away, looking at his body just as she might have regarded it.

Had she enjoyed such lust?

She was pacing now, he could hear the footfalls as they wandered to and fro in the other room. Softening his breath, he sat very still, wishing morning would come and he could dress and they could thrash out what to do about…everything. The quiet turn of paper alerted him to the fact that she was reading the book Lian had given her.

A journal, he thought, for in the second he had held it he had seen the name of the edge on the spine.

August Fournier.

Her father's thoughts. That would not be easy read-

ing. August had been a man ill at peace with his world
or with his place in it. He wished Celeste would wander in to talk with him, to discuss such ramblings. But
she did not, the candle blown out after half an hour and
the dark descending.

He made himself think about the morrow, the routes
they might travel, the dangers they could encounter. Part
of him wanted to turn east on exiting the city simply
because it was the last direction anyone would look for
him. But he had more contacts in the west and south and
he knew he would need them. He also had a good deal
of money now and Lian's help would make the passage
from Paris so much safer.

He wished they were already out of the city and away
on the rural roads. It was easier to hide in the country
than it ever would be in a town filled with soldiers.
Easier to be alone with Celeste, too, but he pushed that
consideration back.

A sniff alerted him to something not being quite
right. Then another one came, muffled by cloth. She
was crying. He hoped it was the book that had incited
such strong emotion and not the regret of lying with
him.

After a few moments, the sound stopped altogether
and then there was only silence.

I am at my wits' end to know what to do about
Mary Elizabeth. I think she is mad and her mother
knows this, too, for she watches her daughter like
a hawk.

Last week she tried to kill us. She fed us meat

*that was laced with a poison and it was only after
a few bites that the Dowager dashed away the
plates so that they crashed upon the floor, table-
cloth and all.*

    *We were sick for days with a fever and Mary
Elizabeth was locked in the West Wing and at-
tended to by a series of physicians.*

    *She tried to kill us again this morning on the
rooftop of Langley...*

Celeste closed the journal. She remembered this. Her
mother shoving them hard from behind with a large
piece of wood so they slipped down on to the icy tiles
and slid a good ten yards before fetching up against
a gutter post that protruded upwards. When she had
looked back, her mama was gone and she and her papa
had finally found purchase to crawl their way back to
safety.

She'd visited Summer in the early afternoon of that
same day, offering her body to the only true friend she
had ever had, in gratitude and in shock. The white and
blue garter she'd worn had been a symbol of all that she
would forfeit in the gesture: marriage, domesticity, a
future. She'd held on to him like a lifeline in a shifting
sea and felt in such sacrifice the first stirrings of grace.

Long gone now, of course, such decency and mercy.
She was everything these days that her mother had
cursed her to be, half-dead and coldly detached. Broken save for this night in Summer's arms.

That thought had her biting down on her bottom lip,
gnawing at the shock of it. She'd begun to feel again in

the deep thrust of his returned ardour, in the warmth of his skin and in the goodness of his soul. He'd leached out some of her coldness and replaced it with hope. Stupid, foolish, inane, nonsensical hope. The misguided desire for a second chance or another destiny that could never come to fruition for people like her.

When Summer had offered her marriage and the protection of his name, as they had both regained their breath after that first time in the barn at Langley, she'd laughed at him. She was tainted with the brush of her mother's madness and not even marriage to Summer would save her from that. It could never have worked between them—demons and angels, after all, were a poor mix.

She'd wished her mother dead then and had returned to the house to find that she had killed herself, the windows being cloaked with dark fabric and the faces of the servants sombre.

She and her father had left Langley early the following morning, running for the English coast and France with all the haste of travellers who had chaos snapping at their heels.

And now here she was again, dancing in the arms of passion and trying to believe it could be more. Until the wedding ring had caught the light of the moon and slashed away any kind of a future.

The saint and the sinner.

There was a truth to the phrase that caught at her last vestige of honour and shattered it into pieces.

Lust required no invested emotion. She saw it merely

as a physical process, a necessary action to soothe the mind and the body. Animals did it. Insects, too.

She shut the journal with a thud, wiped her eyes and lay down to sleep. No more. She must expect only the scraps of intimacy and be happy with it.

She was Brigitte Guerin, murderer, whore and thief, and a woman with the sort of past that meant she could never be more than a ghost on the very edge of a proper society.

Grinding her teeth together, she prayed that she would not dream tonight of the blood of her father's death or of her own shame, so when the touch of Summer Shayborne came into her mind she smiled and relaxed into the warmth of memory. Take this little comfort, she thought, and savour it. Take tonight as a gift, the last joy of intimacy before she walked into the empty wasteland of her future.

Chapter Five

Shay looked through the window, the old glass distorted into waves of blurriness, like his world, not quite real somehow. Until last night, like an onion peeled back layer by layer, he and Celeste seemed to go back to the centre, to the start, exposing the past bit by bit.

He didn't know what came next and this unsettled him, for things were changing in a way he could not quite keep up with and that was a feeling he had seldom experienced.

Footsteps made him turn and Celeste stood there, wiping her nose with the back of her hand as she sniffed, the urchin completely replacing the woman who had come to his bed in the dark hours of the morning, sultry and sensual, her breasts heavy and her lips swollen. There was dirt on her cheeks.

'You rise early, Major.'

Not a question but a statement and said as she walked into the dining room. She carried the bag that Madam Caroline Debussy had given her across her shoulder before unlinking the straps and handing it over to him.

'These are your tools of the trade. The sneaky, clever and unexpected ordinary weapons. I hope for your sake that they can be as effective as a gun.'

Taking the offered bag, he wondered where her firearm was for she had not placed it into the hidey-hole in the apartment in Paris even after promising that she would do so. It was probably in the left-hand pocket of her jacket. Quickly gathered, eminently accessible. But if she was searched, the weapon would be found, and he swore under his breath.

The habits of a spy were pressed into one's soul like a brand. Hers had been a violent apprenticeship and so she'd brought the things she expected to defend herself with. A blade and a bullet.

He turned to gaze again through the window, watching those who passed by the front step and sifting through threat. He knew he should say something about last night, but he could not find the right words and reasoned silence might be better.

'Where's your friend?' Her stress on the word *friend* was cold.

'He didn't come. We won't wait.'

A frown passed across her eyes.

'He's a dangerous man, you know. He's tied to those who sweep through the city for any sign of dissension and snuffs it out without asking questions. There are things said of Aurelian de la Tomber that are not flattering.'

'He works for me sometimes.'

As church bells rang close, counting out the hour, Shay wondered why he might have told her that.

'And you trust him?'

'With my life.'

'Well, it might come to exactly that, Major. There's still a good mile or two until we get to the Seine and if he means to betray you, there is plenty of opportunity for him to do so. Clarke's henchmen from the Ministry of War could be waiting this very second right outside our door.'

She turned to the table and helped herself to a ripe fig, splitting it open. He could see the blush of blood on her cheeks even at this distance. He wished he could not.

'If they take me, Celeste, I want you to run. I will stop them following you.'

'Run like a coward?' She threw this back at him and he smiled because he could not imagine she could ever be such a thing.

'It is worth it for the protection of your life,' he countered after a few seconds. 'I promised your grandmother that if I ever met you on my travels, I would keep you safe.'

'Safe from what, Major. Myself? My grandmother was not inclined to find favour in anything that I did and in the end I gave up trying.'

'She might be surprised by your strength now if you went home.'

'My strength to kill and cheat and lie?'

'I was thinking more of the strength to survive no matter what the world throws at you.'

'As if you know what life has thrown at me, Major.

As if you have even the smallest idea of what my life was like after England.' Now only fury marked her face. 'Susan Joyce Faulkner would hate me a thousand times more now than she did then and she would be right to.'

'The capitulation of the damned?'

She simply looked at him, flinted anger in the vivid blue of her irises.

'I had not taken you for a quitter, Celeste. I thought you might fight for a better life, for a finer future.'

'Not with her. Not like that. Not like before.'

'Then where.'

She threw up her hands. 'Anywhere but England. Anywhere away from fear.'

'Make this the first step, then. Give me your gun.'

'No.'

'No one will be able to save you if you are searched. Not even me. There is no reason for a humble leather worker to hold such a weapon and that is where the danger lies.'

She swallowed, her tongue wetting her dry lips, and he looked away as his body tightened. 'There'd be nothing left to fight with if they take us.'

'Save wisdom, I think. And luck.'

'Poor counterparts to a well-aimed bullet, Major.'

'There is an army behind every soldier. Shoot one and they will all be after us.'

'They already are.'

'But not with such a personal vengeance. Escape depends on good contingency planning and a well-prepared charade. Not reactive force.'

He knew the second she gave in as she reached into

her pocket and handed him the pistol. 'Your protection had better be as robust as it is rumoured to be, Major Shayborne.'

'I promise I will give my life to keep you safe, Miss Fournier, and that your enemies will have to walk across my dead body to get to you.'

He took the pistol in one hand and squeezed her fingers with the other, pleased as the warmth of them momentarily curled about his own. It was odd to be on such formal terms after what they had shared this night.

She wanted to hold on. She wanted to press into him and tell him of all that had happened to her. But she couldn't. Not now. Not ever.

The small, quick connection was as much as she might hope for out here in the no man's land of war, where even a simple mistake could see them both dead.

He looked tired this morning, the scratches she had left on his neck red and angry when he turned to deposit the gun in a box on the table. She hoped they hurt almost as much as she prayed that they didn't.

She wanted to believe that he might drag her through the hundreds of miles of enemy territory to safety without betraying her. The face of Caroline Debussy came to mind and she shook it away, for once the woman had been like a mother to her before she knew the truth of her father's murder. There was no faith left in anything.

'We should go.' She walked away and felt him follow behind her, his silence welcome.

Outside it was warm, the promise of greater heat carried on the wind that blew in from the south. She was wearing too many clothes and the jacket without the weight of her gun in the pocket felt peculiar.

Summer was dressed simply in his tunic, scapular and cowl, the hood pulled back so his face was on show. Watching him, Celeste saw the finesse and the solidness that held him apart from other men. The persona of a Catholic priest was in the kind lilt of his face and in the soft use of his hands, a religious man who walked as though the world was still new and beautiful and there were angels and not beggars on each side of him.

The children of the streets were numerous this morning and his kind face brought them to his side. There was no sign of the soldier, no hint of a man of war and espionage.

He humbly held out the last of the bread he'd taken from his bag and shared it whilst reciting a verse from the Bible.

'For I was hungry and you gave me food, I was thirsty and you gave me drink, I was a stranger and you welcomed me.'

She could hear the accent of the western mountains in his French today. His feet were bare and his nails were dirty. The stubble of two days lay upon his jaw and upper lip, catching all the colours of light.

But Summerley Shayborne was so much more than he seemed. There was a solidity about him and an innate goodness.

A group of soldiers further up had the urchins scattering. 'May God go with you,' he called after them, his hands held together now under his chin in the sign of prayer as the men approached. 'And with you, too, brave sirs. I pray that out of his glorious riches he may strengthen you with power through his Spirit, so that Christ may dwell in your hearts through faith.'

He was rustling through his bag now, bringing out the faded portrait of her father's ancestor. 'In the name of the patron saint of St Barbara, I invoke success and protection so that your journey will be a kind one and a safe one and you will return home unscathed into the heart of your families.'

'We thank you, Father.' The first soldier said this, his smile wide and genuine. Each man bristled with weaponry which made a strange contrast to the homespun plainness of Shayborne's priestly persona, yet he held them in the palm of his hand as he blessed them with charity, compassion and love. And then they passed, hailing a man further on, the street before them empty once again of threat.

'Do you ever doubt yourself?' Celeste's voice shook because the fright was still there embedded in her skin, ice cold with fear. She seldom allowed herself to come so close to any soldiers.

He looked only perplexed. 'This street has a cathedral and two small chapels, and when one operates within the boundaries of the expected there is seldom trouble.'

'And further on? What happens then?'

'We change into the next characters that make sense, allowing no chance of connection to the ones whom they see today.'

'Because they might be able to remember us?'

'No. Because they will. See that boy there, the one with the street urchins who lingers and watches us?'

She nodded.

'His hands were softer than the rest and he did not reach for the bread with the same desperation as the others. He will report to his master tonight of our presence and that man will report to his handler at the very latest on the morrow. He will have seen which door we hailed from and after that it will be an easy leap from obscurity to recognition.'

'They will find the gun?'

'Aurelian will have taken that already and cleaned down the rooms. What will be spoken of is all the things that were not done. We did not pray at the cathedral. We did not take a bed in the house of the Lord for the night or attend a mass. What is expected is always more powerful than what isn't and any digression will lead to questions.'

Celeste glanced at the sky. A little after eight in the morning. The sweat trickled between her breasts and soaked the lawn of her camisole beneath her armpits.

'Which way should we go, then?' Suddenly she felt afraid.

'Which way would you go?' The question surprised her.

'Towards the south. They would not expect to find us heading there.'

'Very well.'

He handed her the skin of water and she drank because the day was becoming hotter by the moment and because suddenly all she could think of was his large body against her own in the night, taut, muscled and warm.

'We will be safe, Celeste. Don't worry.'

She could not say to him that the reason for her frown
was the memory of those hidden hours beside him, of
those moments of being suspended into only feeling,
the empty yawning holes of her life filled with something else. Joy, if she might name it, or delight. Usually
sex simply provided a void of feeling and it had been
so very long since she had known these other things.

So she said nothing and allowed him to think that
she was frightened instead.

Twelve hours of daylight at least before they could lie
together again in the safety of darkness. But would he
want to? She had surprised him last night, she had seen
it in his eyes and on his face and in the guardedness that
had covered all his words today. Would he have other
barriers up now, pre-warned as he was and watching?
Would it be fair to go to him again after a difficult day
of evading an enemy? Would she be one, too, for that
matter? An enemy of a different sort, but broken and
fragmented and impossible to make whole again?

She shook her head. She would not survive into the
night if she was not focused and she needed all her wits
around her if they were to reach safety in one piece.

She observed him as he walked and saw how he covered his limp with a gait that swung him from side to
side. A birth defect? An injury long sustained and ac-
knowledged? An impediment so noticeable none looked
for the other hurt beneath. A further disguise.

This was how he had evaded capture in Portugal and
Spain right under the noses of his enemy. By stealth
and cunning and outright bravery. Even now he turned
and smiled at her, the sun on his head showing up the

small new bristles of blond and the depths in his eyes of velvet amber. The fear that had been a constant companion for so many years fell away under his competence, the chance of life shimmering through a curtain of disbelief.

They would head south on the road to Orléans and towards that wide and useful waterway of the Loire. There were barges they could board to keep them out of the public gaze until they arrived at Nantes, the island port of Brittany. The water was deep enough there for the American trade ships to anchor safely up the river and away from the British blockade. Celeste imagined Shayborne would easily be able to pretend to be an envoy of Madison or a citizen of the American states caught up in an unexpected war and seeking safety.

Perhaps they might even be stopped by a British man of war standing out to sea once they had passed out of the river mouth at St Nazaire? She had heard that they were there.

So many questions.

'It will rain again later today and tomorrow as well by the looks of it.' Summer was observing the sky and frowning.

'A hot wet season,' she answered, the talk of weather a neutral topic that at least allowed conversation.

They did not venture close to one another as they walked among the shadows of the buildings and through the archways that led to smaller streets, though every time they touched inadvertently she held her breath with hope.

Then, all of a sudden, he seemed to have had enough

of the awkward silences for he stopped to lean against a wall.

'Thank you for last night, Celeste.'

Of all the things she had expected him to say, that was the last of them.

'It has been a long time since I bedded a woman, you understand,' he finished, truth in his eyes.

'Your wife...?'

'Yes.'

'I have not been so discreet,' she offered this and watched him swallow quickly and look down. 'My husband, others who I might seek information from, those in my way who needed distraction from my true purpose...' She could have carried on, but she did not. The tawdry reality of her years in Paris spoken out loud was shameful and yet it was a necessary truth.

'You use it as a weapon, then? Your body?'

'Sometimes.'

'Last night?'

'No. Last night I just needed to forget.'

'Forget me?'

At that she smiled. 'Perhaps not you.'

'Then I am glad for it.'

And just like that, the shyness between them dispersed and a new strength lay in its place, for he had allowed their midnight tryst some fineness. She could work with that and manage. No mandate had been set to do it again, but neither had it been negated to the lost realms of a mistake.

Gathering their things, they moved on and Celeste pulled her hat down further across her eyes for anonymity and for protection. There was no one watching them, she was certain of it. No one lingered or tarried, no one walked towards them or away with any sense of a purpose other than their own. She would recognise a careful observation for it had, after all, been a part of her everyday habit for so very long, the feeling of scrutiny was etched into her bones.

'It's clear.' Shayborne's words. He'd been scanning the street as well then and had reached the same conclusion. It felt good to walk with someone else like this, a double protection, another set of eyes.

She saw them half an hour later, two lesser agents of Les Chevaliers, standing outside a tavern on the corner of Avenue Bois de Boulogne and the Place de la Pompe. She was walking behind Shayborne and was glad of it for otherwise he might have noticed the shock that consumed her. Had she been far enough back so that an enemy would fail to place the two of them together? Could he still stay safe even if she was not?

Stepping away into one of the dark alleys to her left, she saw them both change direction and come her way, the washing lines and melee of people separating her for this moment. She welcomed the wet slap of cloth and the pushing humanity of those in the street. If she could get to the river bank, then she would be safe, the water at her feet and the wide countryside before her.

But there were more of them at the next junction. Four others at her count and she knew then that she was in deep trouble. Part of her wondered whether she should even bother fighting, or should she simply give herself up to the inevitable. Without a gun in her pocket she had little chance of escape and she did not wish for the innocents about her to be caught in the violence of a capture. Like the Dubois children had been.

Was this her punishment for the years she had lied and cheated and deceived? A small family moved past her and the fight in her was snuffed out. She waited for the knife or the bullet almost with calmness as she shut her eyes. A quick end and Summer would stay safe. She hoped he would take the rosary to her grandmother as she had asked him.

Then the major was standing there, tight fury beneath his smile and blood on his knuckles.

'Let's go.'

'Where are they?' She glanced around and saw not one of her stalkers.

'Gone.'

She felt him pull her along, his fingers bruising her skin, the cries of people behind them fading as they turned a corner. He looked furious.

'If you are not going to put up a fight, at least do me the courtesy of staying somewhere close so that I can do it for you.'

The dizzy fear that had consumed her made her nauseous and near tears. She had let in hope and the dry taste of it felt bitter on her tongue. Better not to care. Better to be isolated and alone as she always had been for so very long.

'Thank you.' She hated the breathlessness in her voice as she leaned against a door, knotting her shaking hands behind her and frustrated with the way she had handled herself. She was ashamed at her incompetence. Her mind flew now across an escape route and Paris was a city she knew well. 'It is a half mile to the river. They will expect us to make for the bridge. If we turn towards the city wall, they may not follow.' Celeste was pleased after such appalling ineptitude to offer at least a solution for escape.

She saw then that he had different clothes in his hands. A jacket and a shirt. When he peeled off the habit he wore trousers beneath, though his top half was bare and well muscled after all his years of soldiering. With speed he donned the shirt and tucked it into his trousers, handing the jacket to her.

'Take off yours, too, and put this one on instead. Give me your hat and turn your old jacket inside out before wrapping it around your waist.'

He had done the same with his habit, rolled it into a wad of cloth and knotted it about him. The rope from his belt was formed into a rough coil and hung around his arm, like a fisherman might carry the tools of his trade, the hat jammed tight across clipped hair. Sucking at the blood on his knuckles, he lowered his hands.

It was the soldiers, Celeste was to think later, the ones who had passed them by so closely earlier. She had been rattled badly by them and had not recovered, the dreadful fear clawing at memory and leaving her breathless and brittle. At times like this in Paris, after meeting soldiers at a close call, she'd retreated to her apartment for days, curling into fragility until her usual steel returned and allowed her a resolution.

Here, she did not have such luxury. Here, she had to face her next enemy right on the heels of the last one, barely enough time to take in a breath.

Even after all these years the military smelt the same, she thought. Bitter. Pungent. Sharp. The softer scent of Summerley Shayborne rose to calm her. Caroline Debussy's herbs. The ale he had consumed in the house of Aurelian de la Tomber was there, too, and the soap her father used. A mix of lavender and lemon.

Masculine. Safe. Familiar.

She swallowed away the lump in her throat and knotted the jacket. Out of Paris she would cope better. Her fingers fastened on the weighty butt of her knife in the pocket of her trousers and she clung to the steel with all that she was worth.

Celeste looked pale and shaky. The girl who had stood there with her eyes closed, expecting to be summarily slain, so unlike the woman who had walked into the underground dungeon of Les Chevaliers to save him that the shock still stung. Who was Celeste Fournier now? Which version of her was real?

He knew she kept a knife close in her pocket for he could see the tension in her left arm. Beads of sweat rose on the skin above her upper lip and her eyes looked glazed.

Fright, perhaps, he surmised, or memory? What had happened to bring her so easily to her knees in the face of a danger that was far less than the daring of her risky dungeon raid?

He weighed his options and made a decision, pulling her into a doorway a few hundred yards further on and tapping out a code.

The man who answered shut the portal firmly behind them as they came in. 'De la Tomber said you might come.'

'Is he here?'

'No. Last night he arrived late and said there was a possibility you might have need of a room. You and the lad are to have the chamber at the top of the house. I'll send up some food.'

The key was in his hand and then they were climbing, just the two of them, the small room situated among the rafters high above the street. The glass was so dirty he could barely see outside. For further protection, he thought, and pulled the curtain, waiting until the gloom settled into vision.

'We'll stay here until we know more about what's happening. Someone will find us other clothes to wear.' The doorknob was under his fingers.

'You are going out?'

'Just for a short time. Don't worry, it's safe.'

She'd sat down now, her hands either side of her splayed out. Like an anchor.

'I am sorry.'

She didn't elaborate, but he knew exactly what she meant.

'Get some sleep.' He could hear the irritation and shortness in his words as she looked away, her frown deepening, but he did not feel like being kind. He left before the pooling tears spilled across her cheeks.

* * *

It was full dark when she awoke and Summer was sitting on a chair by the opened window looking out towards the sky. He was dressed differently again, a crisp white shirt tucked into snug breeches, the leather boots below well polished. She went from sleep to wakefulness in a second and tried to gauge the time of night from the moon's position.

Not as late as she thought. Somewhere around midnight perhaps? The empty silence of this part of Paris was unsettling. It almost surprised her when he finally spoke.

'They think we have crossed the river already. From the information I have gathered, it is in the area of the cathedral at Saint Lambert they will now be looking.'

'This information is to be trusted?'

'As far as a good measure of gold will allow.'

'And Aurelian de la Tomber?'

'He's the least of our worries.'

'You knew him then, before Paris?'

'In school at Eton. We met when he was being bullied by those who just needed someone to pick on and who didn't care for his French accent. He's been a friend ever since.'

'He's a soldier like you?'

He shook his head. 'A diplomat. Trying to play both sides of an impossible game and coming up short in both camps. I told him to get out of it years ago, but he has…stuck. His father's family is here and I suppose he does not want a repeat of the Terror when anyone with money and lineage in Paris was dragged from their house and murdered. Or at least, he wants to have a warning of it so that he can get them out. That's what conflict comes down to sometimes. A personal fear and a vested interest as a way to protect those you love.'

'Is it the same for you?'

He shook his head. 'There was only ever one reason in it for me.'

'England?'

At that he reached for a glass she had not seen before, raising it to the moonlight so that the numerous shapes reflected back into the room. Crystal, she supposed, and of good quality. 'For all of her faults and for all of her glory, there is no place like home.'

A dig at her perhaps, caught without a past, a future, or a place to call home?

'Your home is still in Sussex? At Luxford?'

The stillness in him magnified. 'It is. My brother Jeremy is ill and one day I will need to be there.'

She remembered his older brother. He was tall and thin and he'd coughed a lot. His young wife, whose name she had forgotten, had always looked sad and there had been rumours even back then that they were having trouble conceiving an heir. She said none of this to him, though, the grief in his eyes palpable.

'If you stop struggling, you stop living,' she gave him this truism quietly, one of the sayings that Caroline Debussy had always been so very fond of. When he smiled she flushed, for he was probably thinking of her inane lack of struggle today and was too polite to say so. A woman who might give advice and yet take none herself. Tiredness swept in about her.

Summer would one day be a lord. Viscount Luxford. He stepped further and further away from her grasp with each and every thing he told her.

'Aurelian said the day after tomorrow is the best day to leave Paris. There is some sort of celebration that the military will be involved in which will keep them occupied, so we will lay low here until he sends word. He also brought us wine. It's a fine white from Cabarets, outside the walls of the city.' He lifted up both the bottle and another glass.

Celeste recognised the flavour as she took the first sip and her mind sifted back into memory.

'It is good.'

'Different at least to the dry whites of Paris and no excise tax either.'

Summer told her this just as memory clicked. Once, she and August had sat on a painted barge on the Loire and watched the sunset each night for a week, drinking this same brew until they had finally made their way back to Paris. Once, August had been a good father. Once, he had been exciting and gentle and kind, until he had been buried under a bitter elixir of deceit and lies.

Then the zealousness had taken over and he had forgotten all the things that should have been important to him. Including her.

Shay had been watching her for a good hour before she'd woken and knew the broken restlessness of her slumber. In sleep she looked softer, younger, less prickly. She'd removed her jacket before retiring and the lawn of her undergarment had barely covered the outline of her full breasts. When she sat up she'd hauled the thing on again despite the heat, all of last night's intimacy lost in the gesture.

He'd wanted to touch her. That thought was surprising. He'd wanted to feel again what he had before, that desperate relief. The warmth of the night loosened restraint, caught as they were in the heat above Paris. Somewhere he could hear music playing, an accordion by the sounds of it, plaintive and melancholic. He laid his head back against the leather rest and asked his question.

'Do you think there is a reason behind everything that happens?'

He saw a half-smile. 'I used to.'

'What changed?'

'Life, I think. Hardship. Death. Now I think it's all random and if you are unlucky enough to be in the place where the world falls in on you, then that's just how it is.'

'Fatalistic?'

'Realistic.'

She said this without even a whisper of doubt.

'I remember you told me once that you wanted to be a writer.'

She breathed out and stood, moving towards the window and looking across the city rooftops.

'You are probably the only person in the world who knows this about me.'

'I kept the story you wrote. The one you gifted me for my eighteenth birthday.'

'A tale of two sisters. One good and one evil. I used to imagine myself as the commendable sister, the one whose life ran along the path of righteousness, but now…' She stopped and placed her palm on the glass. When she took it off, the frosted warmth of skin left a mark into which she wrote her initials. C.V.F. Celeste Victoria Fournier. Another thing he remembered about her, the two sides of her heritage.

'I panicked today. I have never done that before and it worries me, because if it happens again it will be too dangerous for the both of us and I would not want…'

He stood and took her hand and the same sense of shock he had felt last night seared through him again.

'The dangers are there anyway, Celeste, crouching and close, no matter what we try to do to lessen them.'

She was soft and unresisting as he drew her in, the smell of her familiar as he found her upturned mouth and claimed the warmth. Elemental and uncomplicated. Everything was peripheral and far away save for the longing welling up inside.

Slanting the kiss, he came in harder, demanding things she had not surrendered yesterday, the breath of her mixing with his own, a woman who was an enigma and a chameleon.

It was not love he could call on after all these years of separation, he understood that, but what was left was enough.

'Lie with me, Celeste. Please.' Whispered under his breath, the saying of it caressed the skin at her throat.

She did not pull away, but neither did she help him. Today she was compliant, with a quiet sense of consent. He stripped off her jacket and it tumbled to the ground, leaving the wispy lawn in its place, the darker tones of her areolas easily seen through the loose weave of the fabric. His mouth closed over the left one, wetting the cloth, feeling his way as her head tipped back, the veins in her throat almost transparent under her pale skin.

One finger came up to measure the beat, the rhythm tripping fast along the slender and fragile column, though bruising was also visible there. He shook the reality of it away and concentrated instead upon the demands of his body.

He'd always been so very careful and correct, but now he was neither. This was undeniable, the roar of something in his blood that he hadn't felt there before, unguarded and heedless.

He wanted to be inside, in her centre, where they could be joined under another law, a different edict that negated all he had thought proper. The craving in him burnt caution into ashes, argument into acquiescence, and he stripped the bodice from her, firm breasts in the moonlight waiting to be taken.

It was he who did the work tonight, he who covered each nipple and sucked the sweetness from it. He wasn't gentle or tender or quiet, the need in him urging her response, and when he felt her fingers lift his shirt and scrape across the bare flesh on his back, he simply lifted her and took her to bed.

She did lay there, looking up, the colour in her eyes paled by darkness and moonlight, her hair ragged hanks of mismatched lengths, her lips full and ripe.

He had his trousers and boots off and then he tended to hers, the ties knotted fast. Reaching for his knife by the bedside table, he sliced through the tangle, releasing cloth, finding flesh beneath that was hot and ready, one finger slipping into her warmth before reaching deeper.

She did not glance away, but challenged him for more, her legs opening, the movement of their bodies the only thing audible in the silence of the night.

'Lord,' he muttered and closed his eyes, undone with passion. 'Lord knows how I want you.'

Her hand came around him then, around the engorged flesh of his sex, claiming him as her triumph and directing him home.

He positioned himself at the entrance to her womanhood and plunged in.

Afterwards he didn't speak as they lay there cocooned into silence. The great want had been replaced by pleasure, the tangle of her limbs arranged in all the lines of ardour.

He turned inwards to try to find comfort and normality again. He wished she might sleep so that he could slip off without explanation, but he knew she watched him. He could feel the scratches in his flesh where she had risen to his need and let him understand that her own were important, too.

This was no game of unequals.

He had never felt so formless. And neither had he wanted a woman so desperately straight away afterwards that his manhood rose unbidden, throbbing, and when she kneeled and took him in her mouth he leaned back and let her have her way. The groans he stifled with one hand, but he could not dampen the reaction of his body as he spilled himself upon her.

The spoils of war.

Then he lay down against her, wrapping his body around her own and they slept.

She woke to a netherworld, neither day nor night, the heat between them like glue. She could not move for one of his legs lay over her thighs, pinning her to the bed, the hand cupping her breast still in place even in sleep.

Mine, his body said, even in the midst of slumber. She shallowed her breath, remembering the feel of him in all the places he had touched with such tenderness.

They had a whole day to wait out before they could leave, twenty-four hours to attempt to interpret again what was between them. She moved slightly, just a small shimmer of flesh, understanding the power in such a gentle friction, becoming aware when Summer's sleep changed to wakefulness and his big body rocked her own.

She was glad he was behind her and she could not see him, glad when he simply slipped into her wetness without words and took her slowly, the desperation of the night changed into a quiet and certain skill as he angled her hips and penetrated further. Deep and then deeper, she felt the ache of him building until all she knew was the blinding light of otherness, lost in time and space and self.

She closed her eyes and slept, anchored by flesh.

He lay there spent and disbelieving, the day lightening now into warmth, the sounds of the street muffled and the sun dancing on to dusty panes of cheap glass.

The sheets all about them lay in untidy mounds, crumpled with the weight and heat of their bodies. He was glad for the heavy key in the lock and the steel bar beneath it.

No one was getting in or out lest they wanted them to. They were prisoners of ardour and slaves to desire.

His fingers opened and found her centre, the warmth of her sucking him in, the beating pull of her sending him deeper. The other hand lay across her stomach so that he could feel himself inside her, joined together.

'I can't, again...'

He stopped her words with his mouth, taking her answer into his own and rolling across her, heavy with need. There was no other way.

And she knew it.

The ardour in him built and he grabbed her hands so that both arms were stretched upwards, secured against the bedhead.

'Come to me, now.' It was a command and as she rose towards him he took her mouth with his own, understanding exactly what such compliance had cost them both.

He didn't roll away afterwards, but stayed there upon her, a heavy weight of masculine flesh, his fingers clenched around the curve of her bottom.

Chapter Six

It was getting lighter.

He'd brought her water and food, and a clean wet cloth. Celeste wondered if she could ever get back to the woman she had been before entering this room.

She felt drugged by pleasure. She felt empowered and helpless, elated and ashamed.

She had not told him. She had said nothing in the dark watches of the night when he had whispered some of his secrets and she had remained so tight-mouthed about her own.

Summer was afraid for his brother. He was worried about the responsibility of a title. He wondered if he could fit in again to the tight strictures of English society.

Small concerns. She knew he had seen her scars. She had awoken at one time to feel the pads of his fingers running across the faded lines at her wrist.

'We will leave as soon as it is dawn. There is a boat to take us across the river.'

'The celebrations?'

'Will buy us a little in the way of time.'

The coming of a new day meant their lovemaking would be consigned to the dark hours with survival their absolute priority.

She wanted the dawn to linger, to hold them in its embrace, to soothe doubt and allay fear. She wished time would stop now, this feeling of safety so final and complete. But true dawn crept in on quiet footfalls and touched all the hidden spaces of the room, and Summer rose to find them some breakfast.

When that was finished, she buttoned her new jacket to the neck and pulled on a hat that she had not seen before.

He was dressed as a gentleman of means today, his bearing a little bent and a greying wig placed across the short growth of his hair. He, too, wore a hat, an imposing specimen that was almost as fine as the ebony and silver cane he carried.

He so easily slipped in and out of personas, his voice carrying the waver of age as he spoke.

'A carriage will collect us and remove us to the river. We are travelling down the Seine to Les Moulineaux to see my sister who has taken to her bed with an unexplained illness. She is not expected to make a recovery.' Even the slight catch of worry was masterful as he lifted a small leather case and gave it to her. 'You are the servant who will see to my luggage. It is as light as I can make it.'

The last remark was said quietly, his eyes soft with something that she could only interpret as worry. For her. Did he not know that the baskets of bread she often carried as the baker boy weighed ten times as much? It was a new experience to feel wrapped in his care and she found she liked it. It was a weakness, though, for such things could never last.

The carriage was substantial and well appointed. Inside there were small bottles of drink and crusted new baked rolls wrapped loose in calico. They touched nothing as the conveyance moved into the street and the driver called the horses on to a faster pace.

She had expected soldiers but they saw none, the way fast and largely empty. At the river, when the carriage stopped, she let go of the breath she hadn't realised she was even holding because at least in the open there was room to escape.

Then they were on the boat and the ropes were heaved to, the current taking the weight of the small vessel and flinging it south on the Seine out of Paris.

'We'll disembark at the river before it turns north.'

'And go west, maybe? The Americans at Nantes hold a great affinity for the English, despite being a French ally.'

'There's two problems I can see in that, Celeste. If we do somehow manage to avoid being blown out of the water by the British blockade standing out to sea, we will undoubtedly then be heading across the Atlantic to the Americas.'

'It's Spain, then?'

'Well, we can't go north, for odds are they'd think I'd head to England by the quickest route. It's over a hundred miles to Le Havre or two hundred to Cherbourg. To get to the French–Spanish border is at least five hun-

dred and once in Bayonne there is the problem of crossing the Pyrenees in an oncoming winter.'

'A long way and dangerous?'

'It will become safer the further we get from Paris.
Time and distance have an effect of weakening the resolve of an enemy. But it is me they are chasing the
hardest and if you feel you might do better alone...'

She shook her head. There was nothing between
them save the past and that was fractured and difficult. Yet for the first time in a long while she felt she
had found a place, even if only for a short while.

'I won't come back to England with you, but Spain
might do.'

'To live in?'

She shrugged, such vagueness a way of life. Make
no plans. Set no times. Stay in the shadows. Lay low.

'I have good contacts in Santander,' he said.

She nodded and when he did not press her for more
she was grateful. Everything about their relationship
was strange and dislocated. But it was familiar, too,
and it was this that pulled her back and made her want
to stay.

There were weeks of travel before them, each day
holding no certainty. In just three days they had nearly
been killed, shot at, knifed and punched. They'd been
tracked by experts and helped by other shadowy fig-
ures, always contending with the revolution's atmo-
sphere of lies and double dealing. It was hard to trust
anyone in the underbelly of espionage.

Maybe Shayborne did not trust her either. That
thought had her swallowing, for why should he? She

wanted simply to fold herself in his arms and tell him that she would always keep him safe. But she didn't, because how could he believe anything at all that she said? His friend Aurelian de la Tomber had taken the true measure of her. She had seen the dislike in his eyes.

She wished she could have gone back to the moments in the Langley barn again, become that young innocent girl who had laid her virginity out for Summer like a gift. She wished the circumstances of their tryst might have been different. She wished her mother hadn't just tried to kill her and her papa hadn't threatened to leave England altogether come the light of the morrow.

Thrown out.

Those other words echoed across the kinder ones. When she had finally returned to the house to find her mother was dead, her grandmother had exiled her father and called him every name under the sun, her own grief whipping out to include Celeste as well.

'At least leave me Mary Elizabeth's daughter so that I might try to reverse all the damage you have done to her.'

Damaged. Even then.

And here she was again, repeating exactly the same mistakes. Hoping for more.

'Are you ready to disembark?'

She blinked into the light at the sound of his voice and was once again back in the moment.

'There will be horses waiting and we will travel south tonight. The more miles we can cover the better. Tomorrow we shall each become someone else again.'

It was a busy wharf, but there were no soldiers anywhere. The ease of having transport made the transition from boat to land simple and within half an hour they were leaving the river behind them.

Celeste had the thought that she might never see this waterway again, but as the outline of the city against the distant horizon faded, she was not sad. Paris had been her father's home, but it had never been her own. When they turned south it was like shedding another skin, like a cicada, the symbol of a new beginning. She felt immeasurably lighter.

Shay glanced at the time on his fob watch and calculated that they had at least five hours' fast riding before they stopped. That should put them somewhere in the vicinity of Versailles, he thought, which was good because it was a town large enough to be invisible and there would be places to find a lodging. The identity cards they carried would suffice, but Lian had warned him that the checks were more rigorous now. Napoleon's capacity to incite fear, he thought bitterly. Nobody he had ever talked with believed in the wisdom of the Emperor's mission to strike towards the heart of Russia, particularly given winter in the northern lands was known to be uncompromisingly bitter.

Thoughts of the Battles of Narva and Poltava came to his mind, the failed campaigns of ancient defeats suffered in the snow. It felt like the beginning of the end, Napoleon's demise hanging on poor choices and grand pretensions, and today he and Celeste had only just escaped the tail end of it. A crumbling dictatorship was always the most perilous, so many losers scrambling for purchase.

She looked exhausted, the dark rings under her eyes easily seen in such a flat light. But they could not afford to relax their guard, and if anyone had observed them closely today, then they might remember more detail tomorrow.

There was no logic or sense in war, but a thousand different possibilities that could be strung together at any time. Relax, and disaster would follow like it had in the north of Spain, as he and Guillermo had ridden through the olive groves, imagining they were safe.

Four and a half hours later, when they reached Versailles, Shay was more than relieved. It had been a long day after a long and sleepless night and the tavern on the edge of town seemed to suit their purpose exactly.

'Just the one room?' The proprietor was an elderly man and hard of hearing.

'Yes, thank you. The boy can lie on the floor by the door.'

'I'll send up an extra blanket, then, sir, with your food.'

The chamber was small and the bed was, too, a single cot with two grey blankets and two pillows stacked at its foot.

Locking the door, Summer motioned for her to sit, though the movements required to accomplish even such a simple task seemed onerous and difficult. Her bottom stung, her thighs were chafed and every muscle at the back of her neck felt hard and tight.

Celeste prayed to God that they would not be disturbed tonight and that she could just close her eyes and shut out the world until the dawn.

'Here. Have this.' Summer passed her his water canister and she drank from it, the cool liquid making her head clear a little.

'The food will be here soon.'

She shook her head. 'I don't think...I can stay awake...long enough.'

He crossed the floor and kneeled down before her, removing her laced boots with a tug, the hat and jacket following. 'Lie down, then. I will save you some.'

'There's only...one bed.'

'But two blankets and I will be fine on the armchair.'

This close up she saw the shards of gold in his eyes. His hair was growing, too, the light from the window bouncing against the sprouting strands. Gold and white and wheat and cinnamon. No wonder he had dyed it on his journey from the Spanish border for it was so very particularly him.

Her hand reached out and felt the bristles.

'You were always...too beautiful.'

There was puzzlement in his eyes as she lay back and he spread the blanket across her. Then she was fast asleep.

Beautiful? God, he hoped she did not remember telling him that come the morning. Once she had been more forthcoming in confiding in him her every thought, but now she was guarded and careful.

The knock on the door had him turning.

'It's the food, sir.'

A woman's voice and young by the sound of it.

'If you leave it at the door, my boy shall bring it in.'

He did not want anyone to see Celeste asleep in the only bed, for a servant lad had no business at all being there. When the footsteps receded, he retrieved the tray of bread, cold meat and cheese. There was fruit there, too. Fat tomatoes and near-ripe figs.

A thought hit him forcibly that this was the first moment for a very long time that he did not need to be the hero, to act the leader, to order men around or find the perfect and impossible solutions in landscapes full of jeopardy.

No, right now he could eat one of the figs and sit at the window and watch the rising moon for all the hours of the night should he wish it. It was safe here. He knew it was.

Celeste was asleep behind him, cocooned in her blanket, the bruises around her mouth and nose less obvious now and her lip healing. The swell of her breast could be seen above the covering and he pushed down the burst of desire that accompanied such a notice. To-night she needed to sleep.

It was the soldiers who had unsettled her and sent her to fright and he wondered what that meant in regards to her chequered and difficult history. She had removed the bandage from around the base of her thumb and he could see the healing mark of a blade in the shape of the wound.

A further question.

She'd told him she'd seen her father die and that it

was not the English who had done it. Had the French soldiers taken her away at the same time? She had also told him that the world was a chaotic place and if the sky fell in on the spot where you were standing, then so be it. Had the sky fallen in on her?

Once, he had known her almost better than anyone else. And now he didn't. This woman was far more dangerous and unknowable than she had ever been and she was also scared. Of life and love and of all the usual emotions that were part of a normal existence.

She'd used her body like a sharp weapon, prying out the truth of him minute by minute as they had lain together. He'd told her secret fears that he had never voiced to anyone before and such confidence left him hollow, for she'd given him not one single truth back.

Not in words at least. There were other ways he could read people, though, and he knew she was teetering on the edge of a collapse.

He smiled but without humour. It was what happened when after great hardship and difficulty one was unexpectedly freed of it. She'd had a headache when she had lain down for he could see the way her hands shaded her eyes from the light and her fingers had crept to ease the muscles at the back of her neck. Even now in sleep her fingers lay across her forehead in an unconscious protection, yet she had not mentioned the pain or complained of it once.

She woke to the sounds of birds and a breaking dawn and was amazed that she should have slept for so very long. The migraine from yesterday had left her with a dull and aching head, but at least she no longer felt nauseous. Summer was in the chair with one of the grey blankets over his knees and he was dozing.

She felt instantly guilty for having taken the bed for the entire night, so in order not to wake him she didn't move while she took stock of the chamber. It was a plain room but clean. Someone had recently painted it; spots of cream lay on the polished wooden floorboards where the painter had not quite managed a steady hand.

'I know you are awake.'

At that she pushed herself up and leaned against the bedhead. 'Did you sleep at all? That chair hardly looks comfortable.'

'Any soldier learns to take rest where he can and this was more than adequate. How is the headache?'

She was surprised he had known she'd had one when she had been so very careful not to show it. 'Much better.'

'Good. We will leave after you've eaten.'

Celeste felt ravenous at the mention of food and saw sustenance on a stool near the bed. Setting to, she began to devour a fig while pulling herself off a chunk of the crusty country bread with cheese and tomatoes. It was delicious and with the food and a long sleep behind her, her day was shaping up well. But when she saw him wince as he stood to stretch a few moments later, concern ran through her.

'Is it your thigh?'

'It's fine.'

She ignored that and struck on. 'We still have some medicines from Caroline Debussy so I could dress it before we go.'

He hesitated and by doing so she knew that it was far worse than he made out. A sort of unbridled panic made her feel dizzy.

'If you get sicker, we will both be at risk.' Bringing the bag up on the bed, she rifled through the contents for the twists of paper. 'It will be easier to tend to you here than on the road.'

Loosening his trousers, he sat down in front of her, the leg a lot more swollen than she remembered it to be. When she removed the bandage she saw the full extent of the red and angry wound.

'Did they bring salt with the meal?'

'There.'

He pointed to a small dish that she had not seen and she lifted it up to place it on the grey blanket next to him. Water was easy. Mixing them both together in the plate, she poured it across his wound, seeing him tense and grimace as the pain of it set in.

'You need to be staying off your feet with such an injury…'

'Lying around waiting to be discovered? Hardly.'

'If this had happened anywhere else, you would have been in bed for a week keeping it still.' She could hear the irritation in her words, not aimed at him but at the situation they found themselves in.

'The powders helped last time.'

'But I am not a healer like Caroline Debussy. I'm not certain of the mixes.'

'Choose one and dress it with that. Anything is probably better than nothing.'

Celeste looked at the twists of paper and chose the

next shade up from the last one she had applied. This she mixed into a paste with the final dregs of the wine and spread it across his leg, waiting for a moment while the poultice dried before binding it again with a clean roll of fabric.

'I think we need to make for the coast, Major. Six hundred miles of travelling south on that leg no longer seems feasible.'

When he smiled, her irritation melted, the goodness within him as much a salve for her heart as the powders had been for his leg.

'I missed you for a long time after I left Sussex.'

'Between your other lovers?' There was no gentleness in his retort, but she could not be angry. They were her own words to him repeated back, after all.

'And spouses.' She made much of tidying away the powders. She was rarely as forthcoming as she was with him, but the years of distance between them had left a mark that was not easily discarded and lust had only a certain timeframe before its golden edges dulled. Anna was good and sweet and kind and had been his wife for three years. Her few months of friendship culminating in her prickly gift of virginity seemed like nothing in comparison.

A man like him would not be falling at her feet and offering his heart, even should she want him to. And she didn't. There were too many dangers in it, too many unknowns.

'Tonight we will camp in the woods. It will be safer than being in a town.'

Her body warmed at the words. She wished they

were there now, in some secret glade with the stars overhead and hours before them. That thought worried her because sex had always been about gain and business, and this pleasure she had glimpsed was dangerous.

The day outside was a fine one and Summer was as watchful as ever. It was such a welcome change to allow someone else to be vigilant whilst she was lost in the sheer delight of air that smelt of trees and earth and honesty. There was a freedom here that she had not felt in years, a wide and open horizon holding an energy that made her breathe in deeply. Other ghosts of the past slid back, further distanced, less immediate. The aching anger in her bones was weakened by the warmth of the sun and the beauty of the world all around.

'You look happy.' Summer was close now, his horse reined in to walk next to her own on the wider pathway.

'I used to ride in England, but I haven't here. It's nice to be on a horse again. I'd forgotten just how nice.'

'Life makes one forget a lot of things. Remember how we used to race across Langley to see who could reach the river first? I couldn't believe that a mere slip of a girl could sometimes beat me.'

Her laughter floated between them, the audible embodiment of her feelings. 'I seldom did and that was the trouble. Your horse was so much bigger and stronger than mine.'

'But Mirabelle was agile and she could skirt under the trees in a way my mount never could.'

'You even remember her name? My God, I can hardly do that.'

'I remember a lot about those times. The spill you had on the road just before the village comes to mind…'

'Because I bled all over your new jacket?'

'No. Because you were brave and calm even in the face of such an injury. Most other girls would have made more of a fuss.'

'I still have the scar to prove just how brave,' she gave him back, laughter in her words.

'I know, I see it every time we make love.'

Her heart missed a beat and thudded oddly.

History. It both bound them together and split them asunder.

When their horses drew closer she felt his leg against her own and did not pull away, the air between them charged with intention.

It had been like this ever since leaving the tavern, a give and a take, a simmering attraction, another truth under the reality of a simple and desperate desire.

It was as though they lived in a bubble devoid of anyone else where the air was rarefied and thin. All she wanted was to feel him inside her, moving, wanting, needing. All she wanted was for them to stop and make camp and fall into the night.

When the sun finally dropped and the woods became thicker, Summer led her off into the forest. He stopped on the banks of a small stream where the rocks were warm.

'We can bathe here.'

She dismounted and felt her heartbeat quicken.

Her clothes were discarded in a second, a pile at her

feet, and her boots joined them. She had never been a woman who was ashamed of her body and the cool water felt wonderful on her skin as she waded in.

'Hell.' She had not heard Summer swear like this before and turned towards him from her place a few yards out from the bank with question.

'You are the most beautiful woman I have ever seen, Celeste, and the least bashful.'

She was glad he did not comment on the bruises that covered her stomach and back or ask how she had come by them.

This evening was theirs. The bed of nature, the sky, the river, the last birdsong before silence.

'Come in for a swim.'

But he did not, merely taking off his jacket before laying out the bedrolls tied to the horses. There was a stiffness in him that had not been there a moment ago and she wondered at it as she came out of the water, slapping at the midges that had arrived in a cloud with the evening light.

'Your thigh is still aching?'

'Only a little. The powders helped.'

'I will dress it again.'

'Later.'

He moved back, untying other necessities from his horse, tidying things. With the last wisps of the afternoon upon her nakedness she felt altered and powerful as she came across to him.

'It has been a long time since I was out in the countryside and it feels...so very free.' The water from the river had cooled her down and she sensed the regeneration of her soul like a physical thing. The last of the sunbeams warmed her and soft winds whispered. She was like Eve standing before Adam, the forbidden tree allowing them the knowledge of good and evil still far from this moment. In limbo. Caught between time. An exile into isolation and one she wanted with all her heart.

The weariness in him was also apparent, a man who had led her through danger and jeopardy and thought little of his own discomfort. The lines at the side of his mouth were deeper today, more obvious.

With care, she took his free hand and cupped it in the space between her thighs.

'Let everything else go, Summer, for I am right here.'

Opening her legs, she arched her neck, wishing that her hair was still long and falling to the small of her back, wishing that she wore jewellery or perfume or that her face was not marked above her right eye.

He came to her with a frown. She could see the battle he fought to resist her in his eyes, deep amber in the sunset, his golden glance meeting her own. Aroused, rankled and vexed.

Then her nipple was in his mouth, hard and sweet, a lover sustained by her body and fed by want. She could smell herself as he moved, the musk of womanhood, the fresh scent of water.

Basic. Honest. The waves were mounting now, all the parts of her joined in need, pressing for the relief that did not come as he stopped and withdrew.

She felt like falling down to the sun-warmed rocks and was pleased to see him take off his clothes. In the dying day he was unmatched, an Adonis presented to her in the glory of light.

The garden of Eden. The rightness of being here was all-encompassing and as he came against her she knew his urge flamed just as her own did, the hardness of his manhood sliding into the soft wet centre of her femininity. Riding him. Gloriously. Onwards and upwards into the place where the heat burst in upon them both, breathless and shocking, building with wonder before exploding into fragments, the release so acute.

As their breathing finally slowed, he lifted her up and took her back into the river, the cleansing water running across them, soothing their aches.

The night was here now, the birdsong silenced, the small sounds of insects loud in the dark.

When she shivered, he wrapped her in a blanket and lay another on a grassy bank a few yards away.

He did not dress himself, but brought food from his saddlebag, placing it before her as a gift before seeing to the horses, hobbling them so that they would not wander.

When he rejoined her, he had on his shirt and trousers, though his feet were bare.

'I've refilled the water bottle.' He handed it to her, the tiny contact bringing a flush to her cheeks, but it was now so dark she knew it would pass unnoticed.

'I can't light a fire in case it is seen.'

'You think others are close?'

'No. It's just a precaution.'

His glance took in the bodice she now had on, the

heavier shirt unworn. She felt her nipples harden even at his notice.

'I can't stop…needing you.' His words were broken and hoarse, like an apology. They had seldom spoken in the heat of their lust, any words unsuited and out of place. What could they promise each other, after all?

'Then don't stop.'

'And what then?'

It was as if he had read her mind.

'I do not know. I honestly don't.'

An hour later she lay in his arms, the blanket across their shared nakedness as she listened to his heartbeat under her hand. Steady. Solid. Like him.

'I heard once you were in Madeira with your regiment. I could not imagine what it was like there.'

'Hot and colourful. I got sick for a couple of months and spent a good few weeks in bed. The water I think it was and after that I stuck to whisky.'

'And when you got back to England you married Anna?'

'I did. I was lonely, I suppose, and she was kind.'

'Kind and gentle and sweet?'

'All those things,' he gave her back, refusing to be drawn in further.

'Things you liked.' She could not just leave it there.

'Celeste?'

'Yes?'

'There are other things I like, too.'

She smiled as he came in closer, bringing his warmth

with him. She needed to go to sleep, but she couldn't. Everything here had been too wonderful.

'I sent you a letter from Paris. Did you receive it?'

She felt him shake his head. 'Did you send it to Sussex?'

'No. I sent it to your military school in London.'

'You knew I had gone there?'

'Papa said your uncle had told him that you were to attend. I found the address when we were in the city.'

'It never came. What did you say?'

'That I was sorry. That I hoped you would be happy. That I was leaving for France with my father.'

'A goodbye missive, then?'

'It ended with an endearment. I sent you my love.'

She felt him turn as if he were trying to see her in the darkness.

'Whilst fleeing with August?'

'You were always going to be a hero. I knew that even then. Your uncle took me aside one day and told me that you were promised to the young daughter of a friend of the family's and he was hoping for the union. Your parents had spoken of it years before.'

'Anna.'

He said her name in a way that was sad, a catch of resignation there, but he was too much of the gentleman ever to explain it further.

'Word was sent to your grandmother at Langley that you had died alongside your father.'

'It was Caroline Debussy who wrote the letter. She thought it wise.'

'Why?'

* * *

When she turned into him he felt her breath against his chest and her fingers tightened around him.

'Because sometimes people just cannot return to the lives they once lived and it is kinder to give those who wait some closure.'

'The candles burning each and every day and night for you at Langley did not look much like closure to me.'

'My grandmother said that I was as wild as my father and as damaged as my mother. We left before the funeral because she did not wish for us to be there. She said that she could never forgive my father because he didn't love my mother as much as he loved his country.' She stopped for a moment before she whispered, 'And perhaps she was right.'

'Families sometimes tear each other to pieces only out of love.'

'Before Mama jumped she left a note. She wrote to say that I would follow my father and be damned because of it. She said that there was no hope for my future and she could not be there to watch such a tragedy unfold. She said I was wild and selfish and unrestrained. I think my grandmother felt the same.'

'And therein lies the devastation of miscommunication.'

'What do you mean?'

'Your grandmother sent investigators after you a number of times. She had given up on your father, but she paid out handsomely for any word of her granddaughter. The trail went cold in the month of July in

1806 when August wrote and said you wanted nothing more to do with your mother's family. She was desolate.'

Now Celeste turned over so that her back was to him, but he could tell that she was stiff and resistant. Lifting the blanket, he drew his fingers across her shoulders above the flimsy bodice, making circles and letters on her bare skin. He felt the moment she relaxed and was grateful.

'Love sometimes isn't what you say, it's what you do, and Lady Faulkner did do a lot to try and find you again.'

'You like her, then? My grandmother?'

'She is strong and she is a survivor. Does that remind you of anyone?'

Her shoulders shook and he smiled. Reaching into the bag beside him, he extracted the rosary she had given him.

'I won't be needing this again, but perhaps you might. I think your grandmother would be very happy to see you at her doorstep when you are ready.'

'Summer?' He stiffened at her use of his old name. She was the only person who had ever called him that.

'Yes?'

'Thank you.'

Chapter Seven

Celeste woke early the next morning and sat watching the night break into day, the darkness fading to dawn. She tried not to move for she didn't want to wake Summer. Not yet. She liked the silence here. A bird cooed from somewhere nearby and another answered from further away, but there was no human movement, no sound that broke a natural peace with the cacophony of rush or anger or just plain busyness.

The sky looked as though it might be blue and clear today, the cool of night swiftly being replaced by the growing heat of summer.

'Good morning.'

The words came from behind and she smiled, the blanket catching the edges of the movement as Summer tucked it about them.

'I love the peace of this place. In Paris there was always noise.' Even her voice sounded different this morning.

'Where did you live there?'

'Behind the Palais Royale, in one of the small streets to the north.'

'A safety net?'

'A trap sometimes. I used to leave items around to make certain that no one had trespassed upon my territory. Dust from the street, a leaf balanced against my door in an exact position. A hair wound around the handle.'

'Did you ever discover an intruder?'

She laughed. 'A dove once. She ate the breadcrumbs I had foolishly left on the step. She cost me hours of time in worry and it was only the next day when I re-applied the crumbs and waited to see the result that I understood the culprit.'

'You were always careful?'

'Extremely.' She did not temper this word with tones that might minimalise her reply.

'The weight of the damned is a hard way to live.'

'As hard as an English soldier spying in the very heart of an uneasy Paris?'

She had turned now and watched as he tipped his head. 'How long did you live with Guy Bernard?'

'A year.'

'And did he go easily at the end of it?'

'What do you think?' She looked straight at him, his shirt ruffled from sleep, his face indistinct in the half dawn. She could smell him, too, a masculine comforting scent that made her want to breathe in more deeply.

'I think a man like Bernard would not wish to lose any toy that he owned.'

She flinched. 'How do you do that? How do you

see into the heart of a truth so many others would easily miss?'

'I am trained to notice detail. The pinch of a bruise on your left breast. The way he looked at you in the dungeon. The fury when you speak of him which is underlined in fear. How did you meet him?'

'By chance. It was not an easy meeting at all because Papa had just been murdered and I was…barely me.'

'James McPherson said the French soldiers took you…?'

She frowned at that and felt bile rise in her throat, the burn of it making her want to be sick. 'I don't speak of my life much. It's just now, do you understand me? Just here. This second. This moment. This day.'

She felt like striking out at him, hard and fast, a considered blow, a way of stopping more words. But he was turning from her even now, rising, stretching. The muscles on his back rippled with the exertion. Strong, straight and undamaged.

'Men have the better side of war because they can fight back,' she added suddenly, surprised by her own admission.

'As opposed to a woman's lot?' The sound of his words was sharpened.

She made herself be quiet, biting down on the anger that hung beneath the shame.

'It sometimes helps to talk,' he continued and her restraint broke completely as she scrambled up.

'About what, Major? You are only spoiling what is between us with your questions.'

'You don't wish me to know anything more?'

'You know enough. You know more than anybody else in the whole world knows about me.'

At that he smiled, his eyes wrinkling into humour. Sometimes his beauty simply took her breath away.

'When I married Anna I knew that I should not have.'

It was an enormous confession offered without question on her behalf.

'I was lonely. She was kind and honest and good and, whether it was from years of soldiering in harsh conditions or whether it was simply some lack inside of me, these traits became stultifying and choking quite quickly and I could never find the essence of who she was. In the end I gave up looking.'

'Why are you telling me this?'

'Because no one is as heroic as you think they are and because some of your deepest secrets are probably less damning than my own.'

The gift of his truth floored her and she could only watch him as he gathered his things and dressed, too astonished to allow reply. He had not kept loving his wife in the fierce way that she had imagined he had and he felt guilty for it. There was a gift in his admission that was quietly put and it had been a long time since anyone had spoken to her in this way. She respected his honesty and knew that it couldn't have been easy for him to say such things.

The fight left her in a rush and she grabbed at her own attire and pulled it on. She wished he would step towards her but he didn't, his confession building a wall somehow, the disclosure shocking them both. Nothing was quite as it seemed, he was saying. Nothing was written in stone.

Two hours later, her horse threw a shoe so they had to make a detour into the town of Buc, a small settlement some miles off their route. Once there, the farrier told them he could not see to the animal's foot until well into the afternoon and gave them directions to the public house where they could wait out the interim and get something to drink.

Summer looked ill at ease as they sat with an ale in the shade of a tree. The grey wig usually had the effect of lightening his eyes, but this afternoon they looked dark and bruised. Perhaps he still thought of his wife and was wishing he had not breathed a word about their relationship. Perhaps he was confused by her anger and wished himself away.

She liked the warmth of his thigh as it ran down the length of her own on the old wooden seat upon which they both perched.

When she had told Summer that he knew more about her than anybody else ever had it was true. Was this a good thing or a bad thing? Right now, in the shade of a thick, leafy horse chestnut, a kind of contentment stole across her.

I could do this for ever with him, she thought, and was shocked by the realisation.

If Anna's sweetness had been a bane for him once upon a time, then just imagine what damage her own violent chequered past might wreak.

Finishing the last of her drink, she stood, excusing herself to use the outhouse that she could see at the very rear of the garden.

It was an old building with a rickety door and she checked for spiders before entering, seeing only a thick web without an occupant. There was no latch at all so she sat perched above the hole with one hand around the handle, keeping the door barred against any new person who might wish to use the amenity.

A moment later it was snatched away and a man stormed into the small space. With her trousers down she was at a definite disadvantage and as she scrambled up she whipped them back in place as best she could, the seconds needed taking away her own instinctive defence.

'Troy here said he thought you might be a girl?'

'Get out.' She said this quietly, imbuing as much menace as she could in the command.

'You going to make me? The old man you are with don't look like he could hurt a fly.'

'I said get out.'

When he did not leave she simply stepped forward and laid her hand upon the side of his throat, pressing hard. He went down quite gracefully, falling through the door with a quiet ease, but then her own problems truly started.

She felt the blow to the back of her head almost with a calmness, a fist she supposed or something heavier, the dizzy unbalance catching her off guard. Two others had her now and they were dragging her into the bush behind the outhouse, one ripping off her jacket, the buttons popping with such force that everything below was exposed.

She tried to get her fingers around the second man's throat, but he swatted her off and punched her again, this time in the side of the head.

With the last bit of her energy she screamed, a high-pitched cry for help that gave away any last vestiges of her supposed masculine identity. The other man beside her had his hands around her left breast and was scrabbling for more. She bit at his arm with all the force she could muster.

Then Summer was there and he appeared like she had never seen him before. Here was the man legend told of, the soldier and the hero, his face unreadable and indifferent, his eyes almost black with fury.

'Let the girl go.' He stepped in front of her and the lad on her right laughed in his face.

'Who's going to make us do that?' he spat out, dirty fingers squeezing the outline of one breast.

'I am.' Raising his hand, Summer smashed the fellow in the face, grabbing the other one as he went for a knife. A quick kick to the groin had the miscreant kneeling, a discarded piece of wood lying on the ground doing the rest. Even in Paris Celeste had never seen anyone use such damaging force and so elegantly. She was astonished at the pure violence meted out with such careful precision. No wonder he did not use a knife or a gun, his hands were twice as effective as any conventional weapon. She simply stared at him open-mouthed, seeing in his demeanour a thousand hours of practice. Unstoppable and unmatched. A savage and fierce peril.

All the rumpus had others streaming in and among them were soldiers in uniform.

Within a second, he had assessed the capability of the three men to relate a coherent story and found them wanting. Grabbing her by the arm, he led her away through a gate at the far end of the garden before circling around to reclaim their one remaining horse. A moment later, she was on the animal in front of him and they were galloping down the road.

'Will anyone follow us?'

'If they do, we will be ready for them. Are you hurt?'

'I feel strange.' The world was blurring in and out of focus, a ringing sound in her ears that made it hard to hear. It was shock probably, she thought, for the shivers were already coming, her hands barely able to hold on to the edge of the saddle. 'They hit me at the back of the head.'

'I know. It's bleeding.'

'Badly?'

'Scalp injuries always do. If it was bad, you'd be unconscious.'

He stopped her hand as it rose to check out the damage by simply holding on to her fingers and bringing them down inside his own on the reins.

'I think I am going to be sick.'

He'd left the road now to skirt around a thick stand of trees, tipping his head to listen against the wind.

'Someone is coming and coming fast.'

After he'd helped her down she threw up in some bushes on the side of the pathway, clammy sweat beading on her top lip as she closed her eyes to try to regain the centre of things.

The next moment, the hooves of galloping horses were right upon them and then past, three of them by her count. Soldiers, she imagined, her identity and his discovered in the most unlikely of circumstances, for no one watching Summerley Shayborne dealing with those men today could have failed to understand that he was not the old gentleman he seemed.

Her head was becoming clearer, though, as the nausea dissipated and, if she was still shaking badly, she at least thought she might well live.

Summer had discarded his wig, the hairpiece lying strangely in the hook of a shrub's branch. He'd also torn the sleeves off his jacket so that it was a working man's jerkin he now wore.

'We probably have fifteen to twenty minutes until they turn around. There is a track through the fields just there. We will use that. Get on the horse, I will walk behind you.'

'We can't both ride?'

'No. There will be observers, I should imagine, even in this unpeopled part of the world. If we gallop through together, they will see us clearly. This way we can find other byways, less used and more out of the way. *"From each point one finds oneself there are a thousand other ways to travel."* My father used to say that all the time and he was right. Are you well enough to stay in the saddle?'

'Yes.'

* * *

An hour later, Shay thought that they were probably safe. For the moment at least, though there was still the worry of identity cards and a cordon which undoubtedly would be erected around any means of escape. It was also a long way off until the darkness, which was another problem. A good tracker dog would be able to find them, even though he had made sure to use any ditches filled with water as a way of masking their scent.

Celeste was as pale as he had ever seen her, the bright red blood at the back of her head still streaming. He'd tried to stem it with his necktie, but the wound would not close with her upright stance and movement and right now there was no alternative to travelling slowly.

They'd need the night as well if they had any chance of escape and they would have to ditch the horse. In the groins of the hills behind them were thickets of forest, and if he used these to climb into the next valley and then the next one, they might elude an enemy hellbent on finding them.

Checking the position of the sun, he determined the time to be just after two in the afternoon. There was a stream up ahead, he could hear the gurgling of the water and it was this he made for. He'd let the horse go on the other side of the river and Celeste and he would strike on along the bed. Two diverging sets of tracks would waste time and he needed as much as he could get.

She looked a little better now, less shaky at least, though her skin was still a deathly white.

'We will be fine,' he found himself saying. 'The

countryside here is perfect to disappear into and after it gets dark they will never find us.'

He noticed her hands were red with blood from where she had been touching her injury.

'The flow is slowing, Celeste, and if you leave it alone, I am sure it will stop altogether.'

She glanced at him, her head nodding up and down. He saw the bravery on her face and in the way she sat up even straighter and was relieved.

At the river, he helped her off the horse and watched as she dipped her head and hands in the water. It was cold but effective. After a moment or two there was barely any sign still of blood.

Tying the reins into the saddle, he faced the horse the way he wanted it to run and slapped its rump hard. Within a moment the steed was lost to their sight.

'Now we climb,' he told her and took her arm. He knew how sick she was when she allowed him to help her, for normally she would not have countenanced any such aid.

'My father's journal is gone.' She felt ill with the re-alisation. 'It must have been lost when they pulled at my jacket.'

He stood so still she could almost see his mind tick-ing. 'Was there anything in it that could be damaging?'

'I hope not. It was mostly his thoughts and feelings…'

'About you?'

'No. About my mother.'

'A man who writes confidential things down in a world of secrets is a foolish one. Let us hope no one makes the connection that he was your father for Brigitte Guerin has enough troubles of her own.'

'Guy Bernard is dead. Apart from him I don't think anyone else could guess I was someone else, save Caroline Debussy, of course.'

He turned at that, a heavy frown on his forehead as he lifted the bag and gestured her to follow him.

The river was deep in parts and cold, but she walked doggedly on into the afternoon, pushing up and up into the hills until she felt a disconnection between her body and her mind.

'I...think I need...to stop.' It was the head injury, no doubt, and the loss of blood. She had never been unfit in her life and had traversed the Parisian streets for hours without tiring.

The vortex of darkness surprised her, coming through her vision without warning. One moment she could see and the next she could not, the same roaring in her ears as before. As she fell she reached out to try to hold something, long zigzagged waves broken into light.

He heard a noise behind him, just a quiet expelling of breath, and as he turned he saw Celeste fall softly into a leafy shrub, the branches catching at her body and holding her up. He reached her in a second, extracting her from the greenness and laying her down on the track. Her head had begun to bleed again and, grabbing Caroline Debussy's bag, he shoved it beneath her feet, elevating them.

She came to after a few seconds, her eyes fluttering against the light and her hand rising from the dust.

'I am…fine now.' She struggled to sit up, but he held her down, his hand splayed across her middle.

'If you get up too fast, it will happen again, believe me.'

'This has happened…to you before?'

'Twice. Once in Madeira with the sickness I told you of and another time in the north of Portugal.'

She nodded, wiping at her face with the dirty fall of sleeve. 'If you give me a moment…'

She lay back and closed her eyes, her lashes long and dark against her cheeks. No boy had lashes like that, he thought to himself, and found the canister of water.

'Here. This will help. Take a sip.'

She drank deeply, raising herself on one elbow. The bridge of her nose was badly swollen.

'Can you breathe properly?'

'Only through my mouth. I think my nose is broken.'

'No, it's only bruised. If it were broken, it would bleed more and hurt like hell, too.'

'I hope…you are right.' Her voice was small and flat, her eyes leached of the vivid colour that was so much a part of her.

'I'll carry you. We can't stay here for long.'

She shook her head, but he had her up already, his hands under her knees and behind her back as he lifted her off the ground. She weighed so much less than he might have thought, the thinness of her body disguised by her rounded breasts and bottom.

* * *

His heartbeat was loud but slow as he walked on with her, no sign of fatigue or exhaustion showing anywhere on his body. She felt odd and disconnected, weak and cold. The blood loss, she supposed, and tried to rouse in herself the energy to walk, but couldn't. She knew of no one else in the whole world who would have done this for her, picked her up and walked her to safety. For so many years she had been on her own, by herself, in a city that festered with greed and violence.

It was a wondrous discovery, this, and made more so because Summer was a man who knew some of the depths to which she had sunk and who had seen revenge in the blood on the sharp edge of her blade in the dungeons of Les Chevaliers.

He'd used the long length of his old habit to tie her to him, in a sling of sorts that was both ingenious and comfortable, and even an hour later he had barely broken into a sweat.

Still, the way was steep and the oncoming rain had begun to make it slippery, too.

'I can walk if you let me down.'

He shook his head. 'This way is faster. We need to be as far from the town as we can manage by the nightfall.'

'You'd get further without me.'

He began to laugh. 'Are you suggesting I abandon you here, Mademoiselle Fournier, in the middle of nowhere and bleeding?'

'Anyone else would have long ago. They would have recognised that I was not worth the risk.'

'Your friends must be a motley group, then, if that is indeed the case.'

She felt she should tell him that she had no friends and never had, but the confession was too sad and too pointed so she stayed silent. Even as a young girl she'd not held anyone truly close, save for Summer, she thought, for the few months at Langley.

When the light began to fade he finally stopped.

'We'll camp here until the first light of dawn and then move on. It's a site that will let us see if anyone is coming from all directions.'

And it was as he said, the last light scouring steep hills and showing wide valleys in the distance.

'We can't make a fire, but at least the weather is clearing up and if we find shelter under the larger trees we should stay dry. How's the head?'

'It feels a bit better. The dizziness has eased, at least, and it doesn't ache as much.'

'If you eat, you will feel better still. Have some bread and cheese.'

He brought the food from yesterday's meal out from the bag again. It was delicious.

Afterwards, Celeste lay down on the branches he had broken off to fashion as a bed under a huge tree. The sky had cleared and the first stars were out, the heavens endless and bright out here in the dark.

'If I had not dropped my father's journal, then maybe—'

'No,' he interrupted her. 'They knew us anyway, the

soldiers. I could see it in their eyes for the reports from Paris will have been sent far and wide.'

'Would your friend Aurelian de la Tomber hear of this skirmish, do you imagine?'

'He might and it is certainly a hope. Blois lies to the south on the Loire. If we can get there, I have good contacts and Lian knows of them, too. We could find new identity papers and travel again legally, which would make things so much safer.'

'Are you always so optimistic?'

'Certainly—after every setback I have always found a solution that is workable.'

'How were you caught, then? In Spain?'

'Unexpectedly and with a lot of good luck on the side of the French patrol that came across us. I lost a good friend in that skirmish, though.'

'A friend?' She wished to know more now that he was talking.

'A patriot. Guillermo Garcia. A good man who did not deserve to die like that.'

This was said with a great feeling of loss. She could hear the grief in his words.

'When Papa died I felt the same.'

'You saw August die?'

'In front of my eyes. A knife to the breast. The man who sunk it through his ribs was at least skilled so I doubt he felt it.'

'What happened then? To you?'

'I can't remember.'

Her pupils were small black pinpoints of wrath and

Shay knew she remembered just fine, the same way he could recall every second of Guillermo's murder.

What he could not understand was how she had been allowed to live herself after it, for the layers of espionage were deep and secret in the underbelly of Napoleon's empire.

Unless there had been another reason for her prolonged existence? A darker and more heinous truth began to stir in the back of his mind.

The marks around her wrist worried him, as did her reaction to the soldiers and to the two men at the village who had manhandled her.

Perhaps it was not just a loss of blood that had made her dizzy and disorientated? Even now as she bent to pick up another piece of bread, he could see her hands shake in the half-light. He lay down beside her and looked up at the sky, careful not to touch her.

'Do you know the constellations?' Anything to take both their minds off the death of her father was welcomed.

'A few of them. Aquarius. Aries. Orion.'

'There is Andromeda, the chained lady.' He pointed and was glad as her gaze followed the direction. 'She was tethered to a large rock and left out at sea to await the wrath of the great monster Cetus. But Perseus arrived on his winged sandals and, like a true champion, he went to her aid.'

'Did he save her?'

'Indeed, he did. The monster was turned to stone by the severed head of Medusa that he'd brought with him and Perseus claimed Andromeda as his beautiful bride and queen.'

'From tragedy to farce.'

'You think it so?'

'No one ever escapes so easily. Who tied her up in the first place?'

'Her jealous mother. She was reputed to be envious of her daughter's good looks.'

'Because once she herself had been the fairest in the land?'

He decided to play her at her own game. 'You have the drift of it. No one likes losing what they were once fêted for and all families hold secrets that they would rather others not know of.'

'Mama tried to kill me twice.'

The shock of such words spread through him and Shay measured his response.

'Mary Elizabeth had always been weak. Not physically, but mentally.'

Her fingers found his as he spoke and wound in.

He struggled to find the right words. 'I met her by the pond one snowy winter's day and she was trying to save a kitten who had fallen into the water.'

'Did she save it?'

'No, but she tried. She was kind when she wasn't sick.'

The small laugh heartened him. 'Papa said that of her, too.'

'People are never just one thing. They are usually a mix of good and bad.'

'Even heroes?'

'Especially them. The expectations of others can be exhausting and there are times that escape is the only way of keeping sane.'

'Escape?'

'My uncle wanted me to come home and help Jeremy. He hoped that I would take over some of the responsibility of Luxford, but I couldn't find it in myself to do that. I feel like if I return, my brother will die sooner than he should because he will simply give up. I know I would.'

'So you came to Europe and stayed. That was one of the reasons you came north to Paris, too?'

He nodded.

'And now?'

'I am living all these minutes for what they are and trying not to think of going back.'

She turned and her gaze met his. She was perfectly still as she looked at him. He traced the shape of her nose with his first finger and then the outline of her mouth. She had a small scar on the lid of her left eye under the brow that creased when she smiled and he ran the pad of his finger over it in silent question.

'I fell against a wardrobe and split it open.'

'You don't strike me as a clumsy person.'

'Being a wife blurred the lines. My marriage was one of convenience, though my husband, unfortunately, wished for more.'

'He wanted love?'

'And what is that in a city where each moment could be your last?'

'Futile and impossible?'

Like here and now?

This thought made him falter, but he pushed it away and concentrated instead on the lingering want that burned inside him every time he touched her.

'Why did you not run? Leave the city? Find safety when you had the chance after warning me?'

'Have you ever wanted something so badly that it hurt to think about it?'

'No.'

'Then you are lucky.'

'What was it you wanted?'

She smiled. 'Make love to me, Summer, quietly and carefully and slowly. It will help me to forget.'

A single tear traced its way down her cheek from the corner of one eye and he wiped it away.

'Please?'

This time when they came together it was different from anything that had come before. Sweeter. Slower. More real because she allowed him to see her shadows, crouched in the passion, hidden under lust.

Tonight she was not the dangerous Brigitte Guerin or the arrogant young Mademoiselle Celeste Fournier from Sussex or even the woman who had come to his bed that first night in Paris, hungry and demanding of body. Tonight in the darkness she was muted and mellow and deep and she was his in a way she had not been before.

Tonight he understood her pain because it was there in the kiss they shared. He also understood a sadness that was usually cloaked. He wished he might ask her of it, but knew that he would not.

Taking her in his arms, they watched each other as they made love, slowly and with a quiet gentleness that felt just right.

He didn't hurry, but lingered in the moment, a deep contentment settling, for the gift of closeness and contentment was wrapped in an intimacy that was startling. Shay felt that he could see into her very soul just as she was probably seeing into his own.

They would turn for Nantes after they left the hills of this place and make for the coast. Celeste was right that his injury would prevent the longer journey to Spain. He would have to take his chances with the port of St Nazaire and hope that he could find a passage to England.

She would not follow him. He knew that as well.

His hands tightened across hers under the clearing sky, the stars bright in the oncoming darkness, and then he forgot to think altogether.

The port of Nantes was teeming with sailors and tradesmen and passengers. Fishermen were there, too, singing out their catch and hoping for buyers.

They'd come into the town yesterday after catching a barge down the Loire from Blois. It had been an easy journey compared to what had come before. They had slept together every night for almost three weeks under their new disguise of husband and wife. Shay could not remember a time in his life when he had felt so whole and happy.

Last night they had barely slept, holding each other in the darkness with a desperation that was indescribable.

'Come with me, Celeste. To England.'

The small shake of her head had him turning.

'Whatever secrets you keep are nothing to me. You will be safe there.'

He did not mention anything of love because he knew she would not want it.

'One day you will be Viscount, Summer, and a lord. That is your destiny.'

'Then come home with me and be my—'

She placed her fingers across his mouth to stop him saying more, to halt the words that she knew were impossible.

My mistress? My friend? My lover?

She was ruined for anything other than what she was. When he understood that, everything would be easier, but it was becoming more and more difficult to distance herself from the shard of hope that had lodged in her breast. She would never tell him what had happened to her after her father was taken.

Never.

The word sat in her heart like a stone.

Strengthening resolve, firming intentions. She was glad of it, with the feel of his skin beside her and the warmth of his body; magnets which drew her in a direction she could not go.

She had nothing to give him to remember her by, no sentimental piece of jewellery, no keepsake that spoke only of her. It was better this way. A clean break. Another life for him and for her. Memories that were not broken by yearnings. Nothing to tie them. No regrets.

Only a goodbye.

I love you.

The words were there inside her, desperate to be spoken.

I have loved you ever since I can remember. Always.

But she shook her head and remained silent because it was kinder for him and easier for them. Her muteness was the gift he would never know she had given him.

He had risen after this exchange, leaving her there in the bed above the water, and gone up on to the deck. She had not seen him again until the morning when they had disembarked and come into the town proper. He looked tired and tense and sad.

'Lian will be here somewhere.'

'How could he know we are here?' She could not believe in such a coincidence and the cold dread of it shivered across her.

'Because it always pays to have more than one plan in place.'

Different contacts. Other webs. He never ceased to surprise her with the extent of his agents, even in a land that would kill him if the chance presented itself.

De la Tomber had also been there on the day of the Dubois murders. She remembered Guy telling her so.

The threads were twisting again and she hadn't the means to stop it, save in the sacrifice of herself.

'You look pale. What is it?'

'Tiredness. You have kept me awake at night.' The lightness in her tone was as carefree as she could make it and his smile lit the world.

'That is one thing I shall not apologise for, Celeste.'

'Good.'

'You are leaving, aren't you? Now?'

He never missed a beat, she thought. Not even one.

'I am.'

'To go where?'

'Away. A long way away.'

'From me.'

She could not quite voice the lie, so she nodded instead.

'I see.'

Behind him, in the shadow of the town walls, she could see Nolan Legrand and Noah Muller, two of the right-hand men of Mattieu Benet. She knew that there would be others, too, somewhere close. She had spoken to the first two an hour ago when Summer had left her at the tavern and had gone to find Aurelian de la Tomber in order to ascertain which boat he might rely on for a passage to England. When she had met the Les Chevalier agents by the crossroads at the edge of the town, she had given them her troth.

'Take me back to Paris and let the English Major go.'

'Why should we do that?'

'Because I killed Guy Bernard and must answer for it, and because it was Benet himself who ordered the death of the Dubois family. Felix Dubois had been his partner in a business and his death would see great sums of money being transferred back into Benet's accounts. Politics was a cover for greed and one that Mattieu Benet has used many a time. He is out of control and a murderer and needs to be stopped.'

'Liar.'

'Ask Aurelian de la Tomber. He was there. Ask him what was known by Clarke's men and the Ministry of War.'

Muller and Legrand had looked at each other, measuring the weight of the words she had thrown into the ring.

Benet. De la Tomber. Treason. Such allegations, if found to be true, could change the face of the Parisian spy nests for ever and she knew the two men before her were both ready for the chance to lead Les Chevaliers. She had heard them talk. She had noted their ambition. Even Shayborne would be a reasonable exchange for the sort of secrets of which she spoke and the hunger for power was an easy thing to feed.

'I will give myself up without a fight if you pretend you never saw Major Shayborne. He will be gone by nightfall, spirited out of France by magic. Nobody will ever know he was here. You have nothing to lose by it and everything to gain.'

'God!' It was Nolan Legrand who stated this and she knew that she had them.

'But I need to say goodbye to the English Major or he will not go. Then I will return to you.'

'Your farewell shall be in a public place within our sight.'

She turned to look across the square. 'There. Over by those seats and well in range of a bullet.'

'Why would you do this? Why should we trust you?'

'Because I want revenge for the deaths of the Dubois children and I am tired of being ashamed.'

The present moment again returned with a force,

the sound of voices, the slap of water, the smell of fish. When Summer reached over and took her hand she held on with a grief that made her feel dizzy. Their last seconds together. Their final goodbye.

'If you ever need me, Celeste…'

'I will know where to find you.' Unlacing her fingers, she stepped away.

'If you would trust me…'

'I have.' She didn't let him finish, for she knew exactly what he would say.

Fumbling in his pocket for his purse, he held it out, but she did not reach for it. Instead, she turned and walked, one step and then two. When she looked around on the count of thirty he was gone.

She watched the boat leave as she followed Legrand and Muller out of the port on horseback. They had tied her hands to the pommel and Muller led the animal with a care that she appreciated. Not too fast. Not too slow. The white sails of the fishing vessel unfurled against the blue sky, turning in the wind for England, the noise of them lost in distance.

'Please God let him be safe,' she whispered. 'Please let Summer live.'

Chapter Eight

London

'You've come back a damned hero, Shay, and with a new title to boot, though I am sorry to hear of the passing of your brother.'

Lytton Staines, the Earl of Thornton, sat in the seat opposite him, his feet propped up on a leather ottoman. It was mid-afternoon at White's Club and quiet.

'Miss Smithson thinks you are the most heroic man in all of existence. I heard her say it to my youngest sister yesterday. Her cap is set at you by all accounts.'

'She barely knows me.'

'What does that matter? And anyway, your reputation has proceeded you. My advice would be to marry the girl before someone else does, for the Smithson girl is beautiful and kind and the toast of the *ton*.'

'All the more reason to shy away.' He tried to take the harsh edge off his words, but failed. Since being back he'd felt dislocated and splintered. This morning it had taken two hours to be measured for yet another new jacket. He could barely believe the sheer waste of time.

Lian de la Tomber had got him out of Nantes on a fishing boat that had ferried him to one of the British frigates standing just off the coast.

It had been an easy exchange, the reward offered by Wellesley an inducement that the French fisherman and his son had been keen to take advantage of. The captain of the man-of-war lying offshore was known to him and within half an hour of boarding, Shay was heading for England, the French coast receding as he watched from the deck, a cold sea wind against his face.

She would be there somewhere, Celeste Fournier, turning south to look for her own nirvana. Spain, perhaps, or Italy. He could imagine her among the ancient beauty and warmth of such lands, reinventing herself.

Away from espionage, he hoped. Free from the history that had haunted her in Paris. She had tried to give him her father's rosary in those last moments, but he had refused the stewardship.

The acceptance he'd seen in her blue eyes as she'd spoken her goodbye had almost broken him, but he'd been careful not to show her. He was only a small dalliance in the scheme of things, a convenient tryst. All of these truths had lain in the expression on her face even before he'd made for the port and the waiting de la Tomber.

But he had dreamed of her every night since.

The anger in him bloomed. There was no sense in his yearnings and he had always been a logical man. He needed to get on with rebuilding his own life, changed again on the death of his brother, pinning him to the peerage, to Luxford Manor and to an English court that expected him to be solid.

Jeremy had been more than poorly when he had arrived back in England, his fear of coming home only to see his brother die coming true.

'Look after everything for me, Shay. Vivienne will need comfort and I entrust you with that. Make sure she wants for nothing.'

'Your wife will be welcome to stay on at Luxford for as long as she wishes. She will be happy here.'

'And what of you, Shay?' His voice quivered. 'I wish you could be happier.'

'I was in France, Jem.' He took his brother's thin hand and held it tight in his own. 'I met Celeste Fournier there and she was every bit as beautiful as she always was.'

'Then why is she not here? Back with you? Back in England?'

'She could not come. Her father took her into France and chaos and she has been damaged somehow.'

A fit of coughing had ended the conversation and that was the last time his brother had seemed truly coherent. The next day he was dead.

Shay knew that the years of war followed him around like a mantle, too, the myths and legends of battle weaving a story about his endeavours that he barely recognised.

But there was no way to stop them, no way to negate such accolades without exposing the secrets he had always tried to keep safe. The names of other people who had ferried him across a continent sickened by war, the religious affiliates and the less salubrious tittle-tattlers. The blood money of espionage cast a wide net, kept afloat by the endeavours of those who saw in it opportunities for a better way of life.

Morality in a war was nothing like the tepid version of it in peacetime, for more was at stake. He'd felt the breath of death upon his neck many a time as well as the giddy rush of violence. He'd seen men die in all sorts of manners, both slow and quick, and these things could not help but be imprinted on the brain.

He did not fit in here any more for he no longer understood the easy lives of the *ton* or their predilection for gossip. It was over a year since he had last seen Celeste. The scar on his thigh still ached at times and made him think of her touch.

'I think I will retire to Sussex, Lytton. The estate needs tending after the last hard years of my brother's sickness.' Shay tried to keep grief from his tone.

'Come to the Hall-Brown ball tonight with me, Shay. I will pick you up at around ten. It would do you good to enjoy the Baron's stellar wine and some relaxation of spirit.'

Shay had it in mind to refuse, but the look on Lytton's face was so genuine he found himself accepting such an invite. He just hoped his friend would not use the occasion to try to advance Miss Smithson's desire to get to know him better.

Shay spotted Aurelian de la Tomber the second he stepped into the room. He had not expected him to be in London at all and a deep scar across his chin had him frowning.

'When the hell did you get to London?'

'Yesterday evening. I thought to call in to see you on the morrow.'

'I hope it was not your role in my freedom at Nantes that caused you such a wound, Lian.'

'God, you don't know, do you? You do not know of the roiling cesspit your beautiful travelling companion created back in Paris after you left?'

'What the hell are you talking of?'

'This.' He held out his hand and Shay saw half his ring finger was missing, too. 'And this.' The light finally rested on the ruined flesh of his face. 'She came back to Paris and accused the head of Les Chevaliers and me of treason. Surely you had heard? Benet was convicted and he hanged. He was made an example of for the death of the Dubois family.'

'He ordered them dead?'

'For his own benefit, apparently. He was due a good deal of money on the death of Dubois and had seen fit to collect early. Even Napoleon has his limits of depravity, I expect, and with the deepening political crisis in the Empire, there is little leeway to absolve those who break the rules. Henri Clarke vouched for me, though an agent from Benet's coven took matters into his own hands when I was first accused and hence the damage. Les Chevaliers was disbanded subsequently, as were four other deep-level intelligence agencies, so the results of these allegations were far-reaching. The Ministries of War and Police were both well-suited by the total destruction of their competition.'

Such unsettling news left Shay reeling, his breath hitching in shock. Yet Aurelian was still not quite finished.

'When your companion opened her mouth to anyone who would listen, I had a feeling she did not care much about her longevity, so perhaps for her it was a way out, too.'

'And she died because of it?' He could barely ask the question.

'She disappeared, but she is most likely dead. An unmarked grave on the edge of town and the problem of her existence solved. Breaking silence on your superiors is hardly a wise personal choice and the stigma of betrayal is never forgotten, especially if you are a member of the underground groups with their strict codes of loyalty and silence.'

All around the music played, something by the German composer Bach, he was to think later, though at the time he could take nothing extra in. He hadn't left Celeste. She had left him. She had not quit Paris at all, but had returned to it immediately after Nantes to shake up the very basis of the agency she'd worked for. There was no sense in such an action and his anger grew.

'You were in Celeste Fournier's company for a good few weeks, Shay. You must have seen the danger in her?'

Celeste's true name given so carelessly shocked him. 'You knew who she was?'

De la Tomber laughed. 'Her father was a friend of

my father's and I met her years ago. I do not think she remembered me, which was just as well, though she slipped me a blade to use when I spoke with her once after she had made her accusations.'

'What do you know of her father's death?'

'August Fournier? He was killed with a knife to the heart by those whose opinions were different to his own concerning the political future of France.'

'And the daughter?'

'Nothing is known for sure, but it was said that men in uniform took her from the house of Madame Caroline Debussy. The bodies of all five were found a day later, but of the youngest Fournier there was no sign at all.'

'You think she killed them?'

'Perhaps that.'

There was a tone used that made Shay wary. 'Who else, then?'

'She married Guy Bernard a month later. He was a man to whom murder was second nature.'

Shay did not want to take such a conversation further because he could guess all of a sudden what might have happened to the gently brought up young daughter of August Fournier.

'And after she made her accusations, Lian, did you see her again?'

'Twice. She looked sick and thin and broken. But I was hardly offering her my condolences, for her accusations were the sole reason I was hauled up before the council in the first place.'

'God.'

'Who is she to you, Shay? This woman?'

'A friend.'

'A lover, too?'

'Once upon a time.'

The music stopped and a group of people walked over to join them, their laughter so at odds with everything they were speaking of that the moment felt unreal. Lytton's sister, Lady Prudence Staines, was among them and she took Shay's arm and turned him to face Miss Smithson.

'Lord Luxford, may I introduce Miss Crystal Smithson. This is her first Season at court and she has expressed her desire to meet you.'

The girl coloured at such an introduction, but there was no stopping Lytton's sister.

'Luxford needs to learn the art of dancing again. Perhaps he might agree to be your partner?'

Short of rudeness, Shay could do little but smile.

'I have a waltz free towards the end of the evening, Lord Luxford? Could I pencil you in?'

'I would be honoured, Miss Smithson.'

His tone sounded mellow, though he felt only numbness as he watched the girl write his name on a card.

'If you would rather another time, my lord, I would also understand…?'

Having been given an out so prettily and sincerely, Shay shook his head and deep dimples rose from each of her cheeks.

She was as beautiful as Anna had once been, but his jaw tightened as he realised that it was another sort of woman he was seeking, one far from England, far from safety and lost to him in a way he could barely fathom.

Across the room he noticed others observe them and felt a slide of anxiety.

He had changed from a man who saw the best in people to one who only saw the worst. Inside himself now was darkness and a yawning empty desolation. Aurelian's eyes held the same shadows.

He moved aside as Prudence Staines and Crystal Smithson walked away.

'You look preoccupied, Lian.'

'Celeste Fournier, for all her dangerous ways, suits you better than any of these society butterflies. Your past would clip their wings before a month was gone and you would be bored.'

For the first time that evening Shay smiled.

'Join me for a brandy, Lian. In the card room.'

Without further ado, they wound their way across the crowded assembly and made for the quieter quarters to one side.

When Shay left three hours later, the night was full of stars scattered across a clear London sky in the way they seldom were. Endless and uncountable. He wondered if Celeste Fournier might be watching the same sky from somewhere, or whether she had been killed for accusations which had shaken the very fabric of Napoleonic espionage. 'Please Lord, let her have lived.' The refrain caught him by surprise, as did the zealousness of the entreaty.

Celeste made her way north after leaving Paris, travelling on her own and watchful. She did not speak with anyone as she went, dressed as a lad of the land, her shoes worn and her clothes unremarkable. She had found food as she passed through, root vegetables in farmers' fields, juicier fare on the cottage vines of small landholders. She had exchanged her rosary for fish in Beauvais and her crucifix for a gold coin in Amiens. Such trappings of the Lord were well-received and easily pawned. She'd wondered if the sickness she was cursed with would ever go, the nausea and the weakness, the fatigue that ate at her until the thinness made her bones jut out from her body.

She slept in the hedges by day, tucked in under leaves and branches well away from the sight of anyone. She washed in rivers and allowed her hair to grow again, the clipped shortness changing into a length she was able to tie back *en queue*.

She had given Legrand her promise to remain in the rooms he had found for her in Paris after the trial of Benet, but had bolted the first moment his back was turned. She knew what he wanted. She had smelt it on his breath and seen it in his eyes. An easy target, given her accusations. 'I can protect you, my dear,' he had said and she'd known exactly what that meant. She had let nobody near her since Summerley Shayborne and was prepared to kill herself if any man took liberties.

Summer. The name shimmered above everything. He was safe, she was sure of it. Even before she had left Paris rumours were beginning to filter back with the information that Wellesley's greatest spy had returned to his homeland of England. Unscathed. Newly titled.

He would be Lord Luxford now. Aurelian de la

Tomber had spoken the name to her the second time she had seen him, his chin split open like a ripe peach.

'It is just as well that Luxford escaped your clutches when he did, Mademoiselle Guerin.' There'd been no kindness at all in the observation.

'He is a good man with strong moral courage. I wish him well.'

'Unlike you, *mademoiselle*. A woman who might sell her very soul to the Devil if he was paying well.'

'It takes one to know one, I would suppose.' She allowed no hint of softness to be on show. De la Tomber was a friend of Summerley Shayborne's. The two men would meet again some time, she was sure of it, and Celeste wanted no uncertainty of motive concerning her emotions to permeate that conversation.

'Your accusations have made the sort of impact I'd imagine even you have been surprised by.'

'The rot in an apple is never skin deep.'

He had laughed at that and she had seen again a marked resemblance to Summer.

'And you will stay safe?' She had not wanted to utter this, but she had to know. If he died because of her, there would be a new darkness settling around her heart.

'I am a wounded chameleon, but a dangerous one. Do not worry for me. My hands are clean of the Dubois scandal, merely an interested observer for the Ministry of War.'

They had had only these two minutes alone and she had passed him a blade which he had secreted into his pocket in the blink of an eye. Then the Frenchman had been taken away and she had not met him again.

Benet was dead, the small Dubois children's death avenged along with their father and uncle. She hoped Caroline Debussy had been honest in her pledge to help the rest of the family.

Caroline. She had made certain not to visit her, but a letter had come nevertheless, delivered by a street child.

Go to Rome.
Find Monsieur Christian Blanchard in the Piazza Navona.

But she had not imagined she could even complete such a journey with the nausea and weakness she was now afflicted with and so had turned north instead. She had marked a small sheet of paper to keep track of the days as she travelled for time seemed inconsequential and nebulous. Only sunset and sunrise.

Sometimes, though, when she'd lain down to rest she'd had the quiet feeling that she was no longer alone. Sometimes she imagined Summer Shayborne's hand in hers, solid, strong and warm. Almost as though he was there with her.

Chapter Nine

It was getting colder, the summer running down into autumn, the trees in the London parks changing colour. Russets and oranges, reds and browns, the edges of the pathways strewn with leaves.

Lian had accompanied him today on a walk around Hyde Park for it was so much easier to talk there where they were away from listening ears.

'You finally seem to be limping less, Shay. Is the injury easing?'

'My physician says that it is. He said by Christmas I should barely notice the sting of it.'

'So then you will rejoin the army?'

He shook his head. 'The title has made it difficult to simply be up and off as a soldier and Jeremy's wife, Vivienne, is still far from well.'

'The woman I saw you with last week? The one with the brown hair and sad eyes?'

'Melancholy is hard to shake, I suppose, though sometimes...' He stopped.

'You wish she might be braver?'

At that Shay laughed. 'What of you? It seems you are back in England every month these days. Are you still very much involved in things in France?'

'In quieter ways than I was. More in the shadows than the light. The identity card of Brigitte Guerin was found at the edge of the Seine along with some clothes just this summer past. Did I tell you that?'

Shay frowned, not trusting himself to speak.

'Perhaps I should also tell you that Madame Caroline Debussy does not believe Celeste Fournier is dead.'

'You know her? Madame Debussy?'

'She is one of my many godmothers.'

'The sticky web of Parisian society is never simple. What makes her believe this?'

'The girl's forte was deceit and she was an expert in getting people to believe in things that weren't true. She has used up all her lives, Madame Debussy thinks, like a cat, and so she has become someone else entirely to begin anew.'

'And gone where?'

'To ground. To hide. To live her days out in the peace she never had after her father's death.'

'Where do you think she went?'

'I imagine she'd have burrowed into the countryside and made her way south. Caroline Debussy has good contacts in Rome and the rest of the Dubois family have already been taken there. Intelligence insists that it was the fair Mademoiselle Fournier who paid the fare for their transport, so I imagine she would have wanted to see them safe. However, any enquiries I've made quietly have turned up no sightings of her at all. So…'

God. Shay felt sick. Aurelian had said she looked thin and brittle when last he had seen her. The journey south, if she had made it, would have cost her a lot more in energy and resources. He also understood the peril of one who had named her boss as a murderer. Were there others there in Les Chevaliers who had wanted the job desperately enough to help her get rid of Benet? Could they have given her money to disappear?

Questions upon questions. He did not wish to ask his own contacts in the area to look out for Celeste Fournier either, for any notice was dangerous and if by chance she was hiding…?

But the Continent was a big place and a woman travelling alone was easy pickings.

For the hundredth time he wondered why she had not come back with him from Nantes when a passage could have so easily been arranged.

'You have become more bitter, Shayborne, did you know that? You looked different with Mademoiselle Fournier.'

'This has nothing at all to do with her.'

'Does it not? Every time I speak of her I can see your interest. Every time I utter her name you look sad.'

'She is gone. Dead and gone.'

'So you will die along with her and just give up? I have been hurt and disfigured and tried as a traitor in a city that was desperate to blame someone for the imminent collapse of an Empire. But I survived. Now I just want peace and a family. I think I deserve this and you do, too.'

Such a confession made Shay ashamed. Lian was a

good man and a gifted spy. Those two character traits probably had made his life hell and at thirty-three he wanted to settle down, to be quiet and content.

'I have bought a property about an hour away from yours in Sussex, Shay. It is old and beautiful and I wish to make it home. Compton Park holds a great reminder for me of some of the manor houses I remember in Normandy. Substantial and solid buildings that have stood the test of time. Now, perhaps, I can marry, though my attractions are probably questionable and finding a willing bride might be difficult.'

'You have calmed governments and doused the early sparks of international war. I am certain convincing a girl of your finer points would not be too onerous?'

The resulting laughter was heartening and Shay clapped his hands around the shoulders of his friend as they walked on.

In bed that night, he dreamed of Celeste Fournier. He saw her watching him by the river the evening after escaping the soldiers, her hair damp and the shortness of the light brown curls darkened into longer wisps.

'Do you believe in angels, Summer?' she had asked him quietly and he shook his head.

'Well, if you don't I shall disappear.' When he laughed she had simply curled up into smoke, leaving him there empty-hearted.

He'd woken in a sweat because even he understood that dreams like this could be a sign of the truth. Was she dead already? Had he believed in her enough while he'd had the chance to? Lian's description of her being thin, brittle and sick was also a part of his anxiety, for as he sifted back across the dream she'd been the same. Barely there, skin and bone, the mark around her wrist reddened and distinct.

Ropes.

Someone had tied her up. Lian had said that soldiers had taken her. She had been young and beautiful and half-English. He knew what might have happened to such a one in those circumstances and he turned his face into the pillows to try to block his suppositions out.

The last year without Celeste had been the most difficult one in all of his life. Granted, he had lost her once before, but then he had not truly known her, her spirit, her grit, her soul.

He had heard rumours through the intelligence grapevine about the various troubled hotspots in Europe and he had even toyed with the idea of travelling to the Continent to look for her. But she had not accompanied him back to England when she had had the chance in Nantes, so why would she do so now?

Aurelian's confession of wanting to find a woman to share his life with had left a discordant note inside him, too, that threatened to turn everything upside down. For he wanted the same things his friend had spoken of, a family and a home.

He sat up and lit the candle near his bed, watching the light flicker across the ceiling. Celeste had looked so fragile in his dreams, so very easily hurt.

Swearing, he stood and donned his clothes. He would pour himself a stiff drink and find a book in his library. He wished he were at Luxford Manor right now, where at least at first light he could have ridden his horse as fast and as far as he desired in an attempt to escape the demons that clawed at any momentary contentment he felt. But Vivienne was there with all her sadness and needs and the duties of his peerage in London were many and complex.

Trapped.

That word followed him down the stairs of his town house, echoing over and over in his brain. He had never felt so alone.

The last few miles were by far the hardest, Celeste thought, as the horse she had hired passed through the little village by the Manor House of Langley.

The Faulkner family estate, entailed to the son of the house. Her mother's brother, Alexander, was a simple and socially inept man, kept largely in Sussex and in check by his mother. He'd never married. He rarely spoke. Her grandmother had always been the brains and the drive behind both the properties and the title, her son the only one stopping it all being handed over to a distant male cousin. Alexander's affliction had possibly even suited her grandmother, for she had always been a woman with a backbone of steel and had not wanted to lose control of the management of the estates.

The Faulkner country seat. She remembered the land all around her like an ache. The betony and the cat's ear and the red clover. She'd picked bunches of those when she was younger, tying them with twine and presenting them to her mother as a gift when they had come to Sussex on holiday.

The winds were the same, too, gentle and not quite cold, making the leaves twirl and talk. It was so safe here, so very beautiful and predictable. The scudding clouds, the hedgerows, the cottages in rows in the village with their thatched roofs and whitewashed walls. War had not touched this place, had not made the edges harsh and unreliable. A sustainable land of soft promise and quiet sounds. Closing her eyes, she felt her heart beating fast. If her grandmother tossed her out as a harlot…?

But she would not think that. She couldn't. She was glad for the generous warm woollen cloak that covered her. Covered them.

Tying her steed up at a fence post in the front of the house, she smoothed down her skirts, worn from travel and dust and rain. Her hat she readjusted, too, for her grandmother was a woman who put great stock in appearance.

The door was newly painted and the small box hedging around the pathway was neat and tidy. Tidier than it had been when last she was here, the aura of shabbiness disappeared under a new regime of formality.

Perhaps without the chaos of her daughter, Susan Joyce Faulkner had been able to shape her own life with more precision and control. That thought had Celeste swallowing with all that she was about to admit.

With a heavy hand she knocked, stepping back a little as she waited.

A young servant she did not recognise opened the door.

'May I help you?'

On his face dwelt the look of a man who was wondering why such a visitor had not gone to the back entrance.

'I wish to see Lady Faulkner. Could you tell her Celeste Fournier is here? She will know me.'

'Certainly, miss.'

Her voice had probably confused him, she thought, with its accent of wealth and Frenchness. Yet he did not ask her in.

'If you will wait here.'

Inclining her head, she placed her bag of belongings beside her. It looked dirty and small in such surroundings. As dirty and insignificant as she herself looked? she wondered. Repositioning her generous cape around herself, she cradled one arm across the front.

When the door opened again a different and older servant stood in place of the other, a certain avarice in his eyes. She vaguely recognised him as a man who had been here all those years before.

'If you would come this way, I will show you through, Miss Celeste.'

So her name had been recognised and she was not being thrown out on her head?

The inside of the house was just as she remembered it, beautifully appointed and tasteful. In some ways it reminded her of Caroline Debussy's house, elegant and expensive. A gallery of dark portraits faced each other as they traversed down the long corridor to her grandmother's suite of rooms. Faulkners through the ages, all stern as they watched the return of a prodigal and ruined daughter. Both her mother and her uncle's portraits were there, their countenances more regal in paint than they had ever been in life.

A set of French doors opened into the large bed-chamber, light filling the space from windows set along one wide wall.

In a bed at one end a figure sat, pillows stacked behind her. Her hair had been newly combed.

'You have come back, then?'

Not a warm greeting, more of an accusation.

'For now, if you will have me, Grandmère.' Celeste did not move forward, but stood there awkwardly, her voice shaking in a way that she hated.

The French word had the older woman frowning.

'And your father?'

'Papa is dead.'

'How?'

'A knife to the heart. It was quick.'

If her grandmother was kind in her reply, she knew she would cry.

'You may use the lavender suite. Your mother always liked those rooms the best.'

'Thank you.'

'Wilkins.'

The same man as before came again.

'Take my granddaughter to the lavender suite and see that she gets some lunch.'

Then her eyes shut, the lashes thin and spindly on crepe-wrinkled cheeks. Celeste noticed the trace of a single tear leaking from the corner of her closed right eye and turned quickly.

Only a little while. Only until I can get on my feet again. Only if I am welcomed.

The ghost of her dead mother walked along beside her. She could smell the attar of violets she had always used quite distinctly.

Once she was alone, and food and drink had been brought from the kitchens on a tray, she unwrapped her cloak and smiled down at the small child in swaddling cloths, her breasts aching with the desire to feed him.

Loring was five months old and his fingers clutched at her, dark eyes watching as she unlaced her bodice.

'We are safe for now, my love,' she whispered and was glad both for the heavy lock on the door and the large size of the house. She had not told her grandmother of his existence because today she was exhausted and another fight was the very last thing that she wanted. Without Loring, she would never have come back to England. She would have kept the shifting rootlessness of her life on the road on the Continent. But a child changed things, made journeys infinitely harder, and she was willing to risk anything and everything to see him safe.

'I love you,' she whispered as he began to suck, this small scrap of baby taking her breath away with his beauty. He looked like Summer with his light wisps of hair and eyes that had changed from smoky blue at birth into a golden amber. He had the same fingers, too, long and slender.

'I will tell her in the morning, darling, and it will all be fine. I promise you.' She spoke softly in case anyone was outside and because saying the words, however improbable, gave her strength.

Here there was a large, comfortable bed and glass at the windows to keep out the weather. Here there was food and something to drink that would not make them sick. Here if she became ill, others might help her, might help her child. Here there was a measure of security that she had not felt since Nantes.

She knew Summerley Shayborne seldom came home and that he was well occupied in London with politics. She had made it her business to find that out as she had listened to local gossip on her way through the county. He had not remarried either, but that was something she had no right at all to feel relieved about, for she had given up any hope of him over a year ago when she had made her choice to stay in France.

If it was not for Loring, she would never have returned to Langley—she knew that to the very bottom of her heart.

When he finished feeding she changed her son and held him tight until he fell asleep. Then she tucked him in beside her, protected by a cradle of pillows, and covered him with a silky sheet and a fluffy blanket.

They were safe. Sitting back against the headboard, she breathed out, crying noiselessly so as not to wake him. She did not wipe at the tears that fell down her face or try to stop them. She let the sorrow come unbidden, soft against her skin until the fabric of her gown was soaked dark and wet.

For so very long she had not cried. For all the months of her pregnancy and for every month since she had bit-

ten back emotion and carried on. Until now. Until there
was no danger at her heels or sword across her head.

And finally, when the great emotion was past, she
stood and looked out the window, over the fields and
the gardens and the river that ran before the house, the
sun showing up in patches as large clouds raced across
before it.

Home. She had never felt it before but today she did,
the safety of the place wrapped around her, her grandmother, the richness of the decor and the marches of
history. Beside her, Loring breathed fast, the conges-
tion he'd had crossing the Channel so much improved
here. Yet another worry gone.

He looked so perfect, so very solid. The next gener-
ation. Summer's child. Wrapping her arms about him,
she lay back and closed her eyes.

The knocking was getting louder, more forceful, and
as she regained wakefulness, she knew it to come from
the door. With a start, she glanced at the day outside
and thought she could not have been asleep for more
than an hour. Loring was still asleep, though the noise
had disturbed him. She laid a hand across his back and
willed him back to sleep.

Then she answered the door.

The same servant as before stood there. 'Your grandmother requires a word with you downstairs, Miss Celeste. If you would follow me.'

'Just a moment.'

Shutting the portal, she made certain Loring slumbered, piling up pillows all around him to see him safe.

Then, tidying her hair in the mirror and straightening her clothes, she followed the servant downstairs, her heart beating at twice its normal speed.

This time her grandmother was sitting fully dressed at a table in an alcove to one side of a yellow drawing room. She was dressed in an austere navy gown, her hair tightly bound, and she looked so much more like the woman Celeste remembered.

'Please come and join me for a cup of tea. I have a new shipment just in from India. The East India Company imports it and one has to put one's name down months in advance to procure even a small container.'

'Thank you.' Her grandmother's voice sounded feeble and weak, just a ghost of the tone Celeste remembered. She waited as the maid standing behind her moved to pour the tea. The porcelain pot was painted with a variety of exotic-looking birds, their feathers brightly coloured and finely drawn.

'The leaves are ridiculously overpriced, of course, and with the government's penchant of raising the taxes on tea to be able to afford England's expensive wars there is no telling how much higher the asking price will go. In fact, I buy it mostly because Alexander is so very fond of it, but I lock the caddy now so that the staff do not pilfer the leaves, which is rather upsetting.'

As her grandmother rambled on, Celeste found herself bemused. All these words meant nothing. They were fillers in the air with no meaning in them at all save for wasting time. She shuffled her feet beneath the table, a coldness all around her. Autumn in Sussex.

Already the leaves were falling and the first winds had grown cold. Soon it would be winter.

When the older woman dismissed her maid and the door shut behind her Celeste tensed.

Alone now. Just the two of them. The steam from the china cup plumed in the air, the smell of foreign lands on its edge.

'Why have you returned? Why now, after all these years, have you come back?'

The gloves were off and the fight rose in Celeste's throat, only to be squashed down with a true effort. She had no other option, no safety net. The next moments were important.

'I have nowhere else to go.'

'Your mother told me exactly that when she arrived home from France and we all know how that turned out. Badly. A dissolution of the mind. I doubt I can weather another loss of the same ilk.'

'I have a child.' Four words that sat in the air like firecrackers, exploding with consequence and weightiness.

'And the father?'

Celeste shook her head. She could not place Summer's name in the ring of fire.

Her grandmother stood, fingers whitened where they held on to the table.

'How old is it?'

'He is nearly five months. His name is Loring.'

The opaque glance of her grandmother was sharp and she looked each and every one of her seventy-two years.

'He? He is a boy and he is here?'

'Upstairs. Asleep.' Celeste found she could not quite make a full sentence; her mouth was so very dry.

'I see.'

Her grandmother signalled her servant and then without another word she was gone.

Celeste was summoned to her grandmother's room again the next morning, though this time she was asked to bring the child.

Snatching Loring up from where he lay, she changed his swaddling cloth and tidied his face and hair. It never hurt to put on your best face, she thought, as she saw the woman who had come to fetch her watching them.

Her grandmother was in bed today which was surprising, a deep blue shawl draped about her shoulders. When the girl left her in the room and shut the door, the older woman began to speak.

'I am tired today, Celeste, a fatigue that is coming more and more often upon me of late.'

'Then I am sorry for it. I hope you start to feel better soon.'

'Could I see him?' Her eyes were on Loring, tucked up against Celeste's chest and still half-asleep.

'Of course.' She placed her child against her grandmother's raised knees. She had always been a fierce, unpredictable woman and Celeste did not want her son frightened. But she need not have worried, for the lines of sternness disappeared as her grandmother gazed down on her firstborn great-grandson.

'He is beautiful.'

'I think so.' Celeste could not help but smile.

'And bonny, too.' Her grandmother's old fingers caressed his fat ones, though they stilled as the grasp tightened.

'I had forgotten that they did that,' she whispered. 'And the smell.' She breathed in deeply. 'How could I fail to remember that? Loring, you suit your name.'

This was pronounced in the French way with the retracted *L*. 'Does he have other names as well?'

Celeste shook her head, though his birth certificate sported Summer as a middle name. She had not been brave enough to place Shayborne along the line in the courthouse at Calais, so Fournier had stood there instead.

'You are beautiful, little Loring. Where do you sleep, my love?'

'Next to me.' He had done so since his birth.

'Mary Elizabeth's cot is in the attic. Is that something you might wish to use?'

It was the first time her mother's name had been spoken between them, falling as a shared sorrow in the gap.

'It is, Grandmère.'

'Then I shall send for it to be brought down immediately.'

Loring's eyes were fixed on his great-grandmama's, the amber in them obvious in the light from the window.

'Does he have his father's eyes?' The question was quiet.

'Yes.'

'Yet he looks like a Faulkner, too, and it has been so long since we have had the gift of a birth here at Langley.'

Sitting on the chair next to the bed, Celeste relaxed. They had come home, Loring and her, and they were safe. When her grandmother's hand reached out she took it and knew that there was at least a new start in such a gesture. A truce, maybe, and a beginning.

A visitor turned up four days later. Vivienne Shay-borne was small and beautiful. She wore black, the colour suiting her tawny hair, and her eyes were a pale green.

'I hope you do not mind my coming. Your grand-mother had mentioned your presence here and I thought to at least make myself known to you. I seldom have company, you see, so this is a chance to get out of Lux-ford. My husband died a little over a year ago of con-sumption and so...' She left the implication hanging. 'Perhaps you remember me. From before. I recall you vividly.'

Despite herself Celeste smiled. 'I found a brooch of yours once, gold and emerald, that was lost in the kitchen gardens.'

'And you brought it back to me with a bunch of wild flowers. White bryony, if I remember correctly, tied in a blue ribbon. Summerley was a friend of yours, too, was he not?'

Celeste hated the way her heartbeat rose and quick-ened even as she did not answer.

'He has been in London for most of the time since his return from the Continent and, believe me, he has had an enormous impact on the hearts of the young women of society. One of my brother's friends wrote to tell me she swears he will be married soon. Miss Smithson, I think, was the name mentioned, though I have not had time to speak to him directly of it.'

Celeste felt as though the air had left her body. Married. For ever. She made herself listen as Vivienne kept talking.

'The Continental war was a long and onerous one and Shay was glad of some respite from it. Jeremy wished that he, too, might have been a part of the emancipation of Europe, but he could not go.'

'I am sorry for the loss of your husband, Lady Shayborne.' Was this the right title to give her, Celeste wondered, the English system of address so convoluted and difficult?

'Vivi. Please call me Vivi, and whilst I have had a great number of months now to come to terms with it, I suppose that I haven't. May I ask why you cut your hair? I remember it used to fall past your waist when you were here last. One of your crowning glories, I remember it said.'

The quick change of subject was disconcerting.

'It was safer for me to play a lad for a while.'

'On the stage?' Vivienne Shayborne's eyes widened.

'In a war. In Paris. After my father died I became a sort of courier. I imagine that here such things are unheard of, but there…well…I had to live.' She found it hard to finish.

Vivi nodded. 'Sickness has restrictions, too, and my husband and I were not lucky enough to be blessed with children. Your grandmother described your small son in detail to me and I should love to meet him.' Her green gaze rested on Celeste's ringless hands, yet the woman before her did not seem to be here to criticise or to judge. She was lonely perhaps, left in the country as a young widow and trying to cope with her grief. There was melancholy there, too. Celeste recognised such an emotion because she'd often felt the same.

Did Summer Shayborne come to Sussex much? Was he expected home across the coming weeks? So many things she could not ask, dared not ask because she had given up every right to.

'Perhaps you would come to Luxford for tea tomorrow afternoon. I like to sit out in the greenhouse with my dogs when it is fine.'

'I would enjoy that.'

'It's a very quiet house with everyone gone, but the trees are beautiful in the autumn. If you feel up to it, we could have a short walk. I think your grandmother is worried about you. She hoped I could be a friend.'

'She said that to you?'

'Not in so many words, but…'

'Could she come to Luxford tomorrow as well? She may not want to, of course, for she seldom goes anywhere, but I think she might enjoy the invitation.'

Vivi Shayborne clapped her hands. 'Then it will be a proper afternoon tea with the table set elegantly, for it has been so very long since I had real visitors.'

After she had gone, Celeste went to find her grandmother. In the days since she had arrived she had only seen her three times and each time had been different. Yet she had not been asked to leave and treasures had turned up unannounced to her room: the cot and baby clothes, warm winter blankets, a new desk with paper and pens and a fine shawl.

The two gowns she had come to England with had been washed and pressed and mended, and if they were not the pink of fashion, they were nevertheless service-able and presentable. Perhaps it was time to try to work out the future. For her and for her grandmother.

Lady Faulkner was writing in the downstairs salon when Celeste found her, though she hastily pushed the journal under a pile of other papers.

'I am in effect the chatelaine of Langley. Your un-cle's condition has worsened and I need now to put into place other safeguards to protect the estate.'

'Then I hope I am not disturbing you?'

A quick shake of the head was her only reply.

'Vivienne Shayborne has asked us to Luxford for af-ternoon tea tomorrow. She was most hopeful we could both be there.'

A heavy frown crossed the wrinkled brow.

'I saw her yesterday in the village. She said noth-ing of it then.'

'She has just now called in and she seemed very nice.'

'She is a young woman who needs to marry again. Her husband, the Viscount, died a year ago and she has…atrophied here.'

The word made Celeste smile. 'Perhaps she is only now up to welcoming visitors again. She mentioned her dogs.'

'Large Scotch collies. Frightening things. No doubt they will be at her feet where they usually are, drooling and misbehaving. She walks a lot with them through the woods and I have the feeling they need it.'

'Then perhaps I might join her one day for the exercise.'

'You are a nursing mother and I am not sure that would be wise. In my day we simply went to bed and rested and yet still Mary Elizabeth was born a month early.'

That was the second time Celeste had heard her speak of her mother since she had been back. She tried to encourage more.

'That must have been difficult for you to have such a small baby?'

'I had two most competent governesses, so I seldom saw her for the first few years.'

A twist of anger gripped Celeste. 'Well, I intend to be there for every second of my child's life.'

'Even when the censure of others brings you to your knees?'

'I don't need society or its approval.'

The returning laugh was harsh. 'No one lives in a vacuum, Celeste. No one is immune to condemnation and if you think this fatherless child of yours is never going to be called out on such a fact, then you are wrong. My name can give some measure of protection, of course, but after that...'

She turned away, but not before Celeste saw her hands shake.

'I should not have come here...'

She was stopped before she could utter another word. 'Of course you should have come home, for no matter what your father said of me I will always protect family. You and your child will be welcome at Langley until the day I die and beyond it. Know that I would swear such even on my deathbed.'

Celeste was astonished. She had not been asked for the details of her child's father. She had not been castigated for becoming pregnant. Any censure had been directed at those who might be cruel about their situation. Her grandmother was standing between her and condemnation like an avenging angel as she swore guardianship until the day she died.

It was astonishing. In a woman whom Celeste had imagined she would find little compassion, she had received fearsome and unwavering support. Even her own papa had been unable to promise as much.

'Thank you.' The words were small and insufficient, but her grandmother tipped her head and watched her closely.

'If I could give you one piece of advice, it would be this—write to the father of your child and tell him of Loring's existence. You might be surprised by what happens, Celeste, for if my advanced age has taught me anything it is that while one holds on to life, nothing is impossible.'

Impossible.

Some things just absolutely were. For a man of Summer's worth to be tied to a woman like her simply because of a pregnancy was impossible and Vivienne Shayborne had just told her of his interest in one of the most beautiful and lauded daughters of the *ton*.

He could have found her in France, should he have

wanted to, for he had both the contacts and myriad ways of obtaining information. But he had not. He had taken the boat to England from Nantes and forgotten her.

Summerley Shayborne was a good man, a moral man and a hero. Her own mother had had to marry her father because of an unplanned pregnancy and look how that had turned out. They had crucified each other with their unsolvable differences, punishing each other until neither knew any other way to be, even had they wanted to.

She shook away any romantic notion of Summer arriving and professing his undying love the moment he knew she was at Langley. He was probably thanking his lucky stars for such a timely escape.

Life had never been a fairy tale. She could stay here until she worked out exactly what she was going to do and their paths never need to cross again.

The ache of such a realisation almost brought her to her knees, but she had a child to think about and a grandmother two feet away who was watching her carefully.

'I shall not be sending any correspondence, Grandmère.'

'So what is done is done?'

Such words had her nodding. 'It is just us. Me and the baby. There will be no one else.'

Later, walking with Loring across the wide green lawns to the lake, she fell to her knees behind a low stone wall and let the tears fall.

'I will keep you safe,' she whispered to the small sleeping child. 'And I will always love you.'

Another image rose as she said these words, shimmering velveted eyes soft after the throes of lovemaking.

He'd told her she was beautiful and brave on their journey from Paris together, but now he was gone, from here and from her, the lure of London society drawing him in no doubt. She could imagine him in the city with his sense and his calmness, with his ability to negotiate the nuances of language and his easy way of leading people from all walks of life.

Out of uniform he would be war-weary yet tough. How he must have drawn the interest of every lady young and old in court with his danger and mystery!

Celeste picked a wild flower and stripped off its petals, lifting them up in the wind to scatter on the grass before her. She had become superstitious since losing Summer at Nantes and often now balanced one unlucky outcome against another. The way the petals landed. The number of ducks that crossed her path on the way to the river. Sneezing to the right, seeing spiders in the morning, birds flying low in the sky. Every step she took now held the terror of bad omens, the possibility of ill fortune in each living thing coming down to land on her shoulders.

Once she had been brave and certain. Once she had been a woman who walked her world with boldness, daring and fortitude.

Once. With Summer.

She wished he was here with her and their child, and the ache was like a hole that ate at her every day.

* * *

Her grandmother was a completely different woman in the company of Vivienne Shayborne. She laughed at the antics of the hounds and even allowed one of them to curl up at her feet, its long face lying across her shoes.

'I used to have dogs here before my husband died. My daughter played with them for hours and hours, but when one bit her on the hand Walter got rid of them all. No amount of persuasion on both our parts could change his mind.'

'I suppose it's only natural that a father wants to protect his children?' Vivi said this casually, almost as an afterthought, but her grandmother stiffened in a way that was noticeable to them both.

'Protection is sometimes overrated, I think. Better to let a child make mistakes and see the consequences of them. Your husband's aunt, Vivienne, was the perfect example of that, I think. I remember she would allow the Shayborne boys to do the most dangerous things and watch them from a distance. To pick up the pieces, I thought at the time, but now I know it wasn't that at all. She made remarkable men of them both because of her tolerance of their adventurous spirits.'

Vivienne looked entranced at such a turn of conversation. 'My husband was quite tight-lipped about his youth so I should love to hear more of what you know, Lady Faulkner.'

It appeared as if her grandmother would say no more, but then she laid her hands on the table and leaned forward to speak.

'They were little devils, both of them, but in the

most charming of ways imaginable. Summerley, the youngest, was the leader because of Jeremy's fragile disposition, but your husband was never far behind, I can assure you. They built a hut in the woods and slept there for a week once, high in the branches of an old oak. I found the ladders of rope a few months later on a walk and a sign carved into the trunk that read *"Beware of apparitions"*. Not ghosts, as any other young boy might have written, but apparitions. Summerley always had a way with words, even back then.'

'I know that Jeremy missed his brother when he went to the military academy, for he spoke of him often to me.' Vivienne's expression was sad as she said this, leaving Celeste to wonder whether she would ever move on to another marriage, a different life.

'Do you remember the younger Shayborne, Celeste?' Her grandmother now asked this. 'I recall him in the house at Langley a few times before your father took you away.'

'I do.' She kept her voice low and a smile plastered across her face. 'I knew him briefly.'

'Someone turned up here a few weeks ago asking about Major Shayborne, come to think of it. It seems the fellow knew you once in Paris for he left a note. When we get back home I shall find it for you as it had completely slipped my mind with all that has been happening of late.'

Celeste nodded and tried to pretend it was just a trifling communication, but darker thoughts chased around in her head. Loring chose that particular moment to let out a squawk from his Moses basket at one end of the long table and she was glad for the interruption.

She felt the world of espionage sink back into her skin, that certain smell of fear in her nostrils, the chilling knowledge of danger in her heart. A tea party in the middle of the English countryside with laughter and cakes was safe and normal and lovely for others, but not for her.

She was as ruined as they got and as damaged and already the creeping fury of the world that she had lived in for years was coming back, encompassing others, good people, innocent people, tangled in deceit.

'You look pale, Celeste.' Vivienne's voice held concern. 'Perhaps a sip of the lemonade would help. The cook has the tastiest recipe in the whole land, Jeremy used to say, and I do believe that it is true.'

Celeste brought the glass to her mouth once Loring had resettled.

'It's very good,' she said, and the small tête-à-tête continued on, just as if the bottom had not completely fallen from her world.

Later in her room and alone she opened the sealed note her grandmother had finally found for her.

Guy Bernard is alive and word has it he will travel to England in early October to deal with both you and Major Shayborne.
C.D.

The rest of the page was blank.
Caroline Debussy.

He will try to kill you. He will stalk you until he is triumphant. He is consumed with revenge and rage.

Those words could have been as easily written there as the others.

She had not killed Guy Bernard then in the dungeons in Paris? She could scarcely believe her incompetence.

Guy Bernard had not come. Yet. But she could feel that he soon would. His mother's birthday was on October the tenth and she knew he would not miss that. If there was one thing about him that was good, it was the love of his aged mother and his aunt. Today it was the ninth.

The walls of her room seemed to cave inwards, the colour darker than it had been, the windows further away. It was happening all over again, only this time it was all of them who were in the firing line of hatred—the target of a madman.

She needed to travel to London to warn Summer of Guy Bernard's plans. She needed to find him because all this was her fault, her doing.

A knock on the door had her standing and she was surprised when her grandmother waited there.

'May I come in, Celeste?'

Short of being rude, there was nothing else for it but to invite her in and wait until she was seated on the leather wing chair by the window.

'My daughter was a weak woman and my son has shaped up to be exactly the same, but I think you are a strong one. I am glad of it, for I can see the shadows in your eyes and the ghosts that roam in your head. Your father was careless with his political beliefs and I was too forceful with my demands. Between the three of us, I do not think we served you well and I am sorry for it. More sorry than you could ever imagine.'

Speechless, Celeste watched her, uncertain for once of what to say.

'I want you and your child to stay here. I want you to be safe, but I can see already that I have lost you to whatever was contained in that letter, and that you will leave. But I promise I will do everything in my power to help you come home again. *Everything*, Celeste, without fail.'

'I am not who you think I am, Grandmère. The innocent and arrogant girl you knew is long gone and I have done things, been things, that you could not like.'

'In order to live?'

'To survive. There is a difference.'

'When your mother found life tough she gave up. I am glad you are not like her in that way. At least you fight for your existence.'

'I was a spy in Paris as part of an underground and covert organisation. It was not a job for the timid or for the overly moral. It was neither a kind nor a gentle occupation.'

Celeste tipped up her head as she said this, no hesitation in it. If her grandmother would banish her now, then she would not argue. All she wanted finally between them was the truth.

'I sent people to find you so many times in France. I had reports about your father and about his situation, but there was never anything of you. You disappeared from the face of the earth.'

'I became someone else after Papa died.'

'Why?'

'Because I had to.'

'And now?'

Celeste took in a breath. 'Now I need a carriage to take me to London, Grandmère, and I need some lad's clothes, trousers, a shirt and jacket and a hat. Things a serving boy might wear off-duty.'

'A disguise, then?'

'Yes.'

'To deal with the person who brought the letter.'

'No. To try to save a person mentioned in it.'

'And you think you can? Save him, I mean?'

She nodded. 'If I don't, everything will have been for nothing.'

'Then I will summon the butler to aid us. What else do you require?'

Celeste's mind ran across other necessities, but she had some money and she had good weapons. With the element of surprise that might very well be enough.

'Luck,' she said quietly. 'And your prayers.'

'You have them. I don't know what this is all about, but I hope you will come back safe and sound. I would like to name Loring as the next heir of Langley. My son is not likely to make old bones and the place is entailed.'

Shock ran through Celeste. 'You are sure?'

'I am. I have set it down in Alexander's will. There should be no reason for contesting such a succession as long as you swear you were married to his father.

With the losses of war and many civil records being destroyed, we will be able to make it work. It need not be something too onerous.'

Lord, could it work, this scheme of her grandmother's? She had not laid eyes on her uncle since being here, so presumably Alexander was in worse health than he had been when she had lived at Langley before. Another question from her grandmother took her attention.

'Will you take Loring with you to London?'

'No, it is too dangerous. He will need to stay here with a wet nurse and the kindest, most trustworthy servants that you have. I will be back within a week. If anyone turns up at Langley asking for me, tell them that I am dead to you and have been so for a good number of years.'

'Very well.'

'Watch my son for me, Grandmère, and make certain that he is safe.'

'I will employ men from the village as guards. No one will slip in unnoticed. I promise you that.'

When her grandmother stepped forward and wrapped her arms firmly about her body, Celeste rested her head on the top of a bony shoulder and found a peace she had been seeking for so very long.

Lady Faulkner was strong enough to keep Loring safe no matter what happened. Celeste knew this from the very depths of her heart.

Chapter Ten

The English houses of the aristocracy were so well-guarded with their myriad servants and their constant attention to detail. She had been perched across from the town house at Number Eighteen St James's Square for a good few hours now, waiting for Summer to return home, and the dusk was starting to fall.

She knew he would arrive soon for she had spent the morning speaking with some of the servants from the house after pretending interest in obtaining a job there. She had heard that the Viscount was looking to employ a lad to see to the horses and so had used that opportunity to knock at the back door. From there she had begun to chat to one of the kitchen serving girls as she had waited and luckily the girl seemed to have a running tongue and a good deal of free time.

'The Viscount is in the city until this evening when he is to come home to pack for a journey he wil! take on the morrow,' the girl added, 'to call on a woman who he is fond of. There's talk of a wedding soon and all of us are in a tither as to what she will be like. His intended, I mean. Word has it she is a great beauty and very rich.'

Miss Crystal Smithson, presumably, the woman Vivienne Shayborne had also spoken of. She'd left after hearing this piece of news to wait out the hours in a tavern a few hundred yards away and, then, amidst the leaves of a spreading oak in the small park opposite the town house as the day turned to evening.

The Luxford carriage arrived just as she was beginning to think perhaps the information from the kitchen maid had been false, the horses running around the sides of the square in an easy canter and then stopping. Other servants from the house filed out and then Summerley Shayborne stood thirty yards away, dressed in clothes that befitted a titled viscount, his head turned so that she could not get a proper look at his face.

But it was him. The same straight posture, the same walk, though without the limp. His hair was the only thing completely different as now it almost reached his collar in a long wavy mass of blond, his fringe pushed back from his eyes with one hand even as he spoke with the man next to him.

Aurelian de la Tomber.

Stepping back into the greenery, she stood very still. She would have to wait until the Frenchman left for she did not dare to show her face to the one she had mistakenly thrown into danger with her accusations of treachery in Paris. Her fingers wound into the bark of an English oak, feeling its texture, finding a touchstone. Above the city, a small moon began to make its light felt in a sky that threatened rain. Eight o'clock. Her breasts ached with their unaccustomed fullness and the cold of the night settled inside her.

Two hours later de la Tomber left, using the Shayborne carriage as transport to wherever his home was here in London. The lights downstairs were then doused and another moved in a second-storey room, the French doors that led out to a balcony thrown open.

Celeste could not make out any form, save shadow, but presumed this to be the bedchamber of the Viscount. Below the balcony was a wooden lattice firmly fixed to the wall which was raised right up to the second-floor level.

So very easy to climb. This soft world of the English was laughable when compared with all the hidden defences of Paris. Here people lived without expecting trouble, the social norms observed without war tumbling in. The population here gave the impression that conflict would not follow them home and hence embraced their freedoms in a casual way, though from Major Shayborne she had expected more.

When the few other lights below were extinguished she moved forward, glad for clothes that were dark and ones which allowed ease of movement. The footholds were simple and within a moment she was on the balcony, staying still for a moment with her head tipped for any sound.

'Come in.'

These soft words startled her, emanating as they were from the semi-dark.

He was sitting on a chair with his long legs stretched out before him. A single candle flickered on the table at his elbow.

'You knew I was here?'

He ignored her query and formed one of his own. 'Why are you back in England after all this time?'

He sounded distant, indifferent and cold, though the hand nearest the candle shook in the light as he raised it. His hair was tied back now with a leather thing, the formerly careless spill bridled and tamed. The aristocrat was well on show tonight, the political master, resplendent in surroundings that suited him and so far removed from the dirt and poverty of France.

'I have come with a warning. Guy Bernard is on his way here to kill you.'

'You had no need to come. De la Tomber has given me the very same news only this evening, Celeste.' He said her name without any warmth. He said it as though the very sound pained him.

His eyes glanced across her clothing and she was comforted for the hat which covered much of her face and all of her hair.

He did not want her here, she could tell.

'I did not realise Aurelian de la Tomber still maintained such good contacts in Paris.'

'He is in Paris often and has kept abreast of all the happenings to aid his family. It is just as well you waited until he was gone for I am not certain he would wish to see you either.'

'He was there when the Dubois family were murdered. I thought he was involved in it, too.'

'Yet you slipped him a knife after he was taken.'

'He told you of that?' When he nodded she continued, 'By then I understood the true nature of Mattieu Benet.'

'Which was?'

'He had accrued a fortune privately through the blackmail of others, so his scruples were compromised.'

'God in Heaven.'

She frowned. She did not recall him as a man who'd sworn much at all, but, with his face dim and indistinct against the low light he felt like a stranger, like someone she did not know well any more.

'Take off your hat.'

She swallowed, toying with the idea of refusing him completely and then discarding such a wasted emotion.

'I want to see at least just who you have become.'

'I doubt such knowledge could be so easily purchased, Major.' She threw this back at him, even as she reached up for the felt beret.

Her hair was longer now, the same honeyed brown he remembered from her youth, but curlier. It grazed her shoulder blades, thick and glossy, a woman emerging from the plain clothes of a lad. So very beautiful. That thought angered him, as did the fact that his body warmed to her presence like a moth to flame. He knew she had seen his hand shake, but her unexpected reappearance had reignited inside him everything that he had thought dead.

'You never wrote to say that you were safe.'

'Perhaps it was because I wasn't.' Scorn and fury threaded each of her words.

He remembered this so distinctly. This fight and conflict. This anger that had kept him at a distance until she'd wound her body around his own in the darkness and taken every piece of him; poles apart like north and south, yet drawn together by gravity and emotion.

'You must have expected some retribution when you meted out your accusations in Paris.'

'You are right. I thought I would die. I thought that they would kill me quickly and then it would all be over.'

She sat on the floor suddenly, leaning her head against the wall behind her so that a slice of moonlight illuminated her face. This action reminded him so forcibly of their time in her father's rooms high above Paris that he felt displaced and uprooted.

'What stopped you from welcoming death after you escaped, then?'

An expression he did not recognise lay in her eyes, guarded, protective, fierce.

New secrets, he thought. Layers upon layers of them.

'And so you headed south?'

She nodded. 'To Rome. Caroline Debussy has good contacts there. It was comfortable and warm.'

'Lian swears you never reached Italy. Madame Debussy is one of his godmothers and he made it his business to ask her.'

'Where did he say I went?'

'To ground. To hide. He said you were thin and sick

and brittle when he saw you last and that he imagined you were now dead.'

She turned away from the light and reached into her pocket, plainly annoyed by his words.

'If Guy Bernard comes, shoot him. He won't give you the chance to make a second escape.' A pistol he had not seen before sat in the palm of her hand. A beautiful piece inlaid with some shell that glistened in the light.

'I'd forgotten just how brutal you were. Are,' he amended.

'There's more at stake now, Major. Much more.'

'More than even life or death? Now, that is intriguing.'

'It is my duty to protect your back if you will not do so.'

He laughed then, her words so very ridiculous. 'If you are discovered in my bedchamber, Miss Fournier, it might be your reputation that will need protecting.'

'I don't have one. It was lost years ago.'

'In England you are the granddaughter of a woman who garners much in the way of authority and respect. I doubt she would agree with your assessment and believe me when I say that young women are forced into marriage on much less a count than being alone in the bedroom of an unattached male.'

'But you are not that, are you? Unattached?'

'Says who?'

'Everybody I speak to. The *ton* is expecting the announcement of your nuptials to a woman of impeccable credentials any second now.'

'You speak of Miss Smithson?'

* * *

The name jabbed into her heart, piercing her bravado. So it was true, all she had heard. This was not going at all as she had imagined it. Loring's welfare sat in the wings of jeopardy and she needed Shayborne safe. Safe to be a father to him.

For the first time ever she felt distanced from Summerley Shayborne, her actions in Nantes and Paris leaving her caught in his disapproval and censure.

'It is none of my business, of course.' She tried to imbue some sense of apology into the retort.

'You are right, it isn't.'

At that she swallowed and was silent, the quiet stretching on between them into more than a few moments. Finally, he seemed to have enough of it and stood to pour himself a drink. He did not offer her one, though when it looked as if he might cross to her side of the room she flinched. He must not touch her. Her body was different now, changed, and a man of detail such as he would notice. As if he recognised her reticence, he moved back.

'Go home, Celeste, to wherever that might be. I do not need you here.'

'I can't.'

'Why?'

'There are things I have to tell you, things you do not know.'

'Start talking, then. I am listening and this is surely as good a time as any.'

Crystal Smithson's name sat in the room alongside his anger and irritation. Aurelian de la Tomber was there, too, with his hatred and his ruined face. But above them all, Guy Bernard lingered for it was only because of her that Shayborne was being hunted. Again.

It was not the right time to throw Loring into the mix, she thought, her beautiful perfect son who only needed to be loved. So she stood and straightened her jacket.

'I will be here on the morrow, watching over you, and for as long as it takes to know you are safe.'

'I have already refused such help.'

'I know.' It was the only thing she could think to say there in the darkness of a cold London night. When he did not answer she simply walked to the balcony and climbed down the latticed frame under it. Her place beneath the tree opposite would be out of the wind and there she could watch the house for any untoward shadows.

He might not want her, but she needed him. More so now after seeing him again than she ever had before. It was only that simple. She pushed away hurt and uncertainty as she buttoned up her jacket, jerked down her hat and sat among the numerous autumn leaves.

Shay finished his brandy and poured himself another. Where the hell would she go at this time of night in a city she did not know well? He smiled savagely. She was a woman who dissolved into her surroundings. Anywhere might do it. Still, he resisted the urge to watch for her, closing the doors instead and locking them firmly, curtains pulled across the night.

She had left her pistol on the floor next to where she had sat. When he reached down for it her warmth still remained in the metal and he closed his eyes to feel it.

He had seen her the instant he had returned home with Lian, bathed in the shade of the trees. He had always been aware of even the slightest change in his surroundings, long years of jeopardy imprinting such necessity into him. The shock of seeing her had made his world blur momentarily and he was glad Aurelian had not commented on his unease.

He had known she would come up the trellis and in through the doors when she was able. He'd left the lattice there when first he had taken over the house from his brother, reasoning that an easy way in meant he could monitor any suspicious activity. He wondered what Celeste had thought of such laxness when first she had spied the entrance. In Paris the stone walls were unassailable and every apartment had supplementary locks. She would have thought it easy. He hoped Guy Bernard would think the same.

She had looked different. Softer, perhaps, and more filled out. He was glad of it for her sake. She had jumped when he had come closer and he knew to the very marrow of his bones that she had not wanted him to touch her.

Another difference.

The lavender perfume had gone, too, and there had been a scent on her that he did not recognise. Unfamiliar and alien. The anger in him grew.

It had taken him a good year to recover from the loss of her in France. The last few months had been easier, though, more social. Politics had taken the place of the military and he had made himself attend more of the *ton* soirées and balls in all their elegant dysfunction.

Crystal Smithson had become a friend. If she had wanted more than that, she had never mentioned it and he was glad of that. Celeste Fournier's swipe at such a relationship had surprised him. Did others think he was angling to marry the girl? The thought had him frowning.

Lytton Staines had intimated much the same the other day when he had run across him in Regent Street. God, if he was not careful he could wind up married, pining all the rest of his days for another woman and a time when he had felt free.

He crossed the floor and sat where Celeste had sat, viewing the room from that angle. She would have noticed his books, the spines from here easily seen in their neat lines on the shelf. She would have seen the painting of his parents, too, above the bed, which also had him and his brother as boys included in it.

He'd seen her observe it closely, the likenesses well drawn in red pastel and watercolour. A soft and gentle rendering that he had always admired.

Closing his eyes, he leaned his head back just as she had.

What did he want? What did she want? Things had changed between them, time having clawed away ease and comfort. Now they were confused and estranged. He wished he might have the energy to go out into the night to find her. But even in France she had never declared her desire for more than the bedding and her indifference today had suggested she now fancied even less than that.

And therein lay the crux of it all, he ruminated. He'd

wanted so much more when he had returned to England and it had shattered him, leaving him broken and uncertain for months. He could not withstand another round of loss.

He shook his head. No, if she came again he would allow her no glimpse into the hurt she had smote him with. He swore this on the departed soul of his brother.

Loring looked exactly like Summer as a child.

The picture behind the bed had been a revelation. The same shape of eyes and line of nose. The same fairness of hair and length of body. Her breasts prickled at the knowledge and she was pleased she had thought to bind them so tightly. The smell of her milk lay on the air and prompted a desire to hold Loring that was so vital it almost undid her.

Was he happy at Langley? Was he unsettled? Please God, let Guy Bernard be here tomorrow so that I can go back, she prayed.

But Summer needed her, too, and seeing him in the flesh for the first time in fifteen months had brought forth a barrage of feelings.

She wanted to lie with him and tell him all the things that had happened to her, all the hurts and the secrets. She longed to whisper everything she knew of Loring to him, all the small insignificant triumphs and worries that only another parent might understand and savour.

Bernard would be here either tomorrow or the next day, she was sure of it. He would come with his stealth and his anger and he would attack when they least expected it. She had to be ready. She had to be prepared. The gun in her pocket was loaded and primed. All she had to do was to wait.

She was asleep, curled into the base of the tree in a bed of leaves. This uncharacteristic defencelessness was so surprising Shay simply stood there watching her, the sun newly rising in the east over a waking city.

'How long have you been here?' she asked gruffly a few moments later.

'Long enough to have killed you had I been Guy Bernard.'

Unexpectedly she smiled, her eyes brightening. 'Then I am glad you were not.'

'Come and have breakfast with me, Celeste. You look like you need it.'

She stood, brushing the detritus of a night's interrupted slumber from her clothes and when her jacket gaped a little he saw the rise of one breast above a heavy binding of linen. More rounded and full. He looked away before she noticed. 'This protection you insist on giving me is not necessary.'

She said nothing as she followed him into the house. The sideboard in the dining room was laden with fare to break their fast and his servants watched her with more than interest. Today she looked nothing like the lad she was dressed as, and when she took off her hat her hair spilled down, curlier than it had been yesterday.

'If you would like to wash first, there is a bathroom through that door.'

She nodded and promptly disappeared, returning

five moments later with water sluicing down her wild curls and her face washed. She looked more beautiful than he had ever seen her. Shaking away that thought, he gestured for her to sit.

'If you do intend to stay, perhaps I could offer you the use of my library. You once enjoyed books, if I recall?'

'I've barely read in years.'

'And yet people have not stopped writing. There are some recent editions of novels that I could recommend.'

She met his gaze then, full on, and he could see things inside her eyes that he had no words for, hidden dark things brittle with sadness. The servant at her back interrupted such discoveries, though, as he asked her what her preference was for the morning's meal. When she had given her order she once again observed Summerley Shayborne.

'I was sorry to hear about Jeremy. He sounded like a lovely man. I cannot remember meeting him, before.'

'Who told you of his death?'

'Many people.'

That was also a lie for there was complicity on her face. Lord. So many feelings came flooding back. Complex complicated feelings that he had no need of.

'When did you arrive in England?'

'Just over a week ago.'

'Have you been down to Langley?'

He knew that she had even before she answered him.

'My grandmother was pleased to see me. You were right about that.'

'And now? After this? Will you go back to Sussex again?'

'For a little while. Just until I find my feet.'

'I am due down at Luxford next week. Vivienne, my brother's wife, has been despondent since Jeremy's death so I try to see her when I can.'

The bruising in her eyes darkened. She was not pleased with his words. Breathing out, he began to eat his eggs and bacon and she did the same.

The food tasted like dust in her dry mouth. Summer would be in Sussex next week! It was too soon. The wheels of fate were turning too fast and she could stop none of it.

This morning he was dressed down and he looked so much more like the man she had traversed France with, the man she had slept with every night for weeks.

Love me, she felt like saying, here in a room filled with food and servants. *Take me in your arms and make the world right again.*

Swallowing such emotions, she directed her mind to other things and was pleased when he spoke.

'Aurelian said that Les Chevaliers was disbanded along with a few other of the agencies of Napoleon?'

Such a change in topic was welcomed.

'Perhaps de la Tomber may have been happy with such a result. It strengthened the remaining agencies, the Ministry of War included, though I did not stay around the city to be sure of that.'

'I don't think he would have seen it in such terms.'

Celeste caught the edge of something. 'Why?'

'He was unveiled, I suppose, which is a difficult thing to be when you wish to work as a spy. The same might be said of you, Celeste. Being unveiled, I mean?'

'Once that was true.'

'But now?'

'Now I have other more important responsibilities.'

She could see he was more than interested to know what these might be, but was too polite to ask.

'What else did de la Tomber say to you of Guy Bernard?'

'He said he had taken a long while to get back to full strength after his "accident". He also said he was a wild cannon whom no one now had any time for.'

'Which makes him doubly dangerous.'

'I thought the same.'

'Where was his information coming in from?'

'Clarke's office, I suppose.'

'A second source, then. My warning was from Caroline Debussy.'

'And I hold a third. Bernard was seen coming off a fishing ship late last night in the English port of Dover.'

Celeste frowned. 'Then he will be here today.'

'Which is why I want you out of it. I want you gone.'

'No.'

'Your presence will only make the meeting more difficult, given the last time he saw you, you cut his throat.'

He was striving for cold distance and she could not allow it. 'Two sets of eyes are better than one and I can fire a gun with expertise.'

'The bloodthirsty Celeste Fournier?'

'He is dangerous to us.'

'Us?'

'All of us,' she amended and looked away.

'Me. You. Who else?'

'Anyone around us. He will kill anyone at all to get what he wants.'

'And you lived with a man like this?'

'He helped me once. He helped me survive.'

'After your father's death?'

She stood at that suddenly, pushing the chair back so hard it fell over, the noise of it bringing the servants in quickly from the kitchens. 'England is the soft land of ease and excess, Major. There is nothing here that could make you understand exactly what it was like for me there in the middle of a war in France. You could not know how it was.'

He got up, too, his blood running as hot as her own as he grabbed her arm and pulled her from the room. When she went to scratch him with her other hand he fastened on that one, too, lacing her fingers together with his fury. Once in his library he pushed her inside and locked the door.

'Then tell me what it was like for you, Celeste. Tell me what happened after the soldiers took you away from the house of Caroline Debussy; the same five soldiers who were found a day later with their throats cut in a room off the Champs Elysées.'

'You know that?'

'It was Guy Bernard who killed them for you, wasn't it? He killed them because they had hurt you.'

'No.' The croak of the word was barely audible. 'You

can't know this. You were not there. Anyone who was is dead.'

Tears were running down her cheeks now, tears that she did not even dash away as they fell unstopped, a dam of emotion that had suddenly burst.

'What happened to you, then?' This time he was gentler. This time he felt his own throat thicken. 'Tell me, Celeste, and then live, damn it!'

She brought one hand up, running it through her hair, and he could see the conflict of whether or not she should allow him the truth in her eyes. Finally, resolution settled.

'What do you think might happen when five soldiers take a young girl to a private room?'

He'd asked himself the very same question, but was now silent as she continued.

'They raped me for a whole day and all I thought of was you.'

'Me?' He could not quite understand what she was telling him over the loud beat of his heart, over the sound of rushing in his ears.

'You were the only man who had ever touched me like that before…and so I pretended that…it was you until all…I could see was your face and all…I could feel was your body. I could even smell you there, that particular scent that I have never forgotten. Even when I screamed I imagined it was you.'

'Hell, Celeste.' This time he leaned forward and took her in his arms. This time she did not fight and she felt soft and right and warm. She felt like home as they stood together with the horror of the past streaming down her face.

'It's over now. I will see you safe. I promise it.'

He whispered the words into her hair as he held her close, the clock in the corner ticking away the moments and then the half hour.

He would keep the fury of all she had admitted inside him until he was alone, keep it in a place where it was controlled and manageable until he could deal with it in his own way. He kept swallowing away the thickness in his throat.

When she finally pulled back he let her go, but he was not quite finished with his questions, for he needed to know what had happened as desperately as she needed to tell him.

'Then Bernard came and killed them all?'

She nodded. 'He'd heard the commotion for his contacts had alerted him of the soldiers' presence. I did nothing to stop him. I stood there and watched until every one of them was dead and I was glad of it.'

'Good for you. I would have done the same thing. They deserved exactly what they got. Sometimes justice like that is the only punishment for men who have stepped so far outside humanity. Sometimes death is the only option for a depravity that is staggering.'

'Thank you.'

'For what?'

'For listening. For not judging. Even for asking me to tell you because I am certain things like this are easier out than in and I have always thought that it was my fault, or my father's.'

'It's not. I hope like hell that you know it wasn't.'

'I know. Now I know. Before I didn't.'

He swallowed as he gave her his next words. 'I want to talk to Guy Bernard when he comes. I want to have the chance to comprehend this revenge of his, to understand why he has come here now.'

'I tried to kill him. He will never give such retaliation up and I don't want to be looking over my shoulder for ever.'

She looked spent and exhausted. Her eyes were red and her nose was running, but the fear in her face was lessened.

'You won't need to. I will see to that.'

'So what happens now?' Her voice was small and hollow.

'I'll be the one waiting for him to come.'

'No. I want to be here, too.'

'Very well.'

To send Celeste off alone after what she had admitted seemed wrong. 'But you have to promise not to get in the way, not to shoot. Guy Bernard is mine, the final piece in the puzzle of the past. I want you blameless in his death. Do you understand?'

He was giving her the gift of the life she once thought she had taken. He was allowing her clemency. After all she had told him, he would still give her that? She could barely believe it.

'He will come this evening, using the trellis beneath your window. He will wait until it is dark and the house is silent because that is what he taught me to do. If you greet him in the same way you did me, you will have him at a disadvantage.'

The clock in the corner chimed out the hour of eleven in the morning. Had it been that long since breakfast? It felt like hours on the one hand and like no time at all on the other.

'I'll ring for tea. I think we both need it and afterwards the housekeeper will find you a room so that you might have a sleep. It will probably be a long night.'

She nodded, pleased at the way he had taken charge of everything since her mind was still ringing from her confession. Once, she had imagined she might never have survived such an admission. Now all she knew was the relief of it.

He had listened to her words as a man and an honourable one at that. She could have asked for no more and the discharge of culpability was empowering.

Her body was free again and only hers, no longer soiled and tarnished. The grace Summer had given astounded her. She wanted to cross the room and crawl back into his arms, the protection found there so very precious.

But she did not, of course. Tea was coming and so was Guy Bernard, and if Summer had any chance of defeating him, he'd need his mind on the job. Already she could see him thinking in that particular way of his, the spy who had outwitted all his enemies because of cleverness and sharp wits.

'Unload the gun you brought and put it on the table there. Live bullets in a room this size are liable to hit things they are not meant to. Besides, people generally want to tell their story and he will be no exception. But for now, we will have a drink and rest for there are plenty of hours to wait.'

His housekeeper had taken Celeste to the yellow bedchamber, a room that overlooked the back garden and which caught the afternoon sun. Situated on the next floor up, Shay was glad of the distance between them. His body shook with outrage from all she had told him, the fury building until he could stand it no more.

Shutting his door, he drove his fist into the wall beside it, the scrim jagging against his skin and drawing blood and pain, and the sort of ache that finally broke through the blinding anger of what had happened to Celeste.

He drew back his arm and slammed it in again, this time a sob of anguish escaping with the crash and then he hit out a third time, the madness diminishing exponentially with such temper and passion as his more usual resourcefulness crept back in.

He didn't want to break his fingers, he needed the damn things to confront Guy Bernard when he came. Leaning back against the wall, he slid down it, legs folded up, his mouth against his hand, sucking at the bruising and the split skin.

He felt worn out and drained. He felt het up and energised, too, if that was indeed possible. It was how Celeste had always made him feel as she rode upon the edge of danger in everything she did. She was unlike anyone else he'd ever met and that was saying something in his walk of life.

He would deal with Guy Bernard and take Celeste Fournier home to Luxford. He did not care what happened in the future or how difficult it all was. She was his. She always had been his and always would be.

He would protect her and cherish her and keep her safe. Nobody would ever hurt her again. He was willing to sacrifice everything to make certain that this happened.

And so I pretended that it was you until all I could see was your face and all I could feel was your body. Even when I screamed I imagined it was you.'

Celeste challenged him and made him furious. She'd offered him her body even after everything she had been through and filled him up completely with her own brand of passion. Her secrets were dark and heinous, but then so were many of his own, the shady deals of espionage wrought in blood and deceit. He'd killed people, too, under the banner of war and sometimes it had not been pretty.

She was exactly right for him. She made his blood beat faster when she came near and his heart swell with bursting pride.

In her he could only see the grace and the hope of survival. She was the rose that bloomed among the debris, determined, brave and true. The White Dove. James McPherson had the truth of it there.

He laid his hands finally upon his knees and wept for all that they both had lost.

Chapter Eleven

They waited together in the darkened room, not speaking, Celeste's gun drawn against the window as they watched the night sky fade into darkness and the moon rise above the city.

This morning they had felt like strangers, but this evening they were more than that again. Stronger feelings were there, too, but he could not at the moment think about those.

He teased the silk of a scarf he had in his hands through his fingers, the strength of it reassuring. Every part of his body was honed and ready for action.

The sound came an hour later, small at first and then more loudly. Scraping and a footfall. Shay took in a breath and kept it there, not a single thing upon him moving. Still. Readied. Focused.

The shadow of a man and then the body with a blackened face turned to the room.

'Stand very still.'

At Celeste's voice the figure stopped immediately. 'Now step in slowly and raise your arms.'

Guy Bernard stood there now in the light of the candle Shay had struck, beardless, thinner, a smile upon his face. His hands were devoid of weapons.

'Major Shayborne,' he said softly in French, ignoring Celeste altogether. 'So all those rumours from Nantes were true?'

'Rumours?' He could not understand quite what Guy Bernard meant.

'Be quiet, Guy.' Celeste's words showed the steel in her voice, but the Frenchman wasn't listening.

'You do not know of the sacrifice that she made for you?'

'What the hell are you talking of?'

'This.' When he tipped his head Shay could see the scar of her knife's work on his neck. 'As well as her accusations against Benet. It was a pure exchange. Her life for yours. The things she had to say were more important than what might have come from your interrogation, I suspect, and she'd promised to go without fight to Paris if you were left alone to take safe passage back to England.'

Shay glanced briefly around at Celeste, sick with the realisation of the danger she had placed herself in for him. When she refused to meet his eyes he swore, for nothing with her was ever as he thought it and he could see the truth of Bernard's words in her eyes. Sacrifice.

'And now no doubt she is crawling into your bed with all her gifts, a woman who might see her best chance and take it.'

'Enough.'

But Guy Bernard was not ready to cease, not by a long shot.

'Perhaps it might be wise to ask her about some of her other secrets. They are certainly worth listening to.'

'You speak of the soldiers who took her after her father's murder? I want to thank you for your part in seeing to their demise. It was the honourable thing to do.'

That surprised him, a heavy frown on his face settling.

Shay took two steps towards him. 'Why are you here?'

'I want my wife back. I want her to return with me to France. It is her place, after all.'

'An unlikely conclusion to our meeting.'

'She owes me her life. She owes me for this.' His hand again indicated the old wound at his throat. 'We were never divorced in the law courts and any judge in France would back me up on that.'

'You are delusional.' Celeste pushed into the conversation now, no careful diplomacy in what she said.

'Go back to France and never return to England.' Shay spoke across them both. 'That promise is the only way you will leave here alive and I allow it only because of the way you dealt with the soldiers.'

For a moment Shay thought he might go, indeed he made to, his body turning even as the knife was flung. Towards Celeste.

'If I cannot have you, Brigitte, then this Englishman most certainly will not. I swear it.'

The blade hit her in the arm, spinning her off her

chair and sending her tumbling to the floor, a bright splash of red on the rug. Then there was another blade in Bernard's hands as he stepped towards her, his focus only on Celeste.

The scarf came around the Frenchman's throat as Shay bore down upon him, the light thin silk unbreakable and solid. He ignored the heavy thumps against his back and twisted the fabric twice before jerking the neck up, a slight small pop telling him it was finished.

Bernard's inert body fell to the floor, the reddened face frozen in a mask of death as Shay's fingers checked the pulse just to make certain that he indeed did not live.

Celeste simply kneeled there in shock after pulling the knife from her injured arm, her face pale and breath shaky as he moved across to her.

'It's not a fatal wound. You're not bleeding heavily.'

She shook her head hard. 'It is my fault, all this, and you are the one to pay for it…again.'

She was breathing so fast now he could barely make sense of the words. It wasn't the wounded arm that was upsetting her at all, but his part in the demise of Guy Bernard. He held her carefully up against him, his hand pressed down on the injury so that the slow seepage of red would cease altogether.

'Life is never one thing, Celeste, and you of all people must know that. Bernard died for your safety and for your deliverance, and I would kill him again in a second. This had to happen in order for you to live and for me this is honourable.'

Such words seemed to reach her through the mist that was fogging her brain and her fingers came up to his face, tracing the line of his cheek, stopping just short of his lips. 'You are beautiful, Summer, both inside and out.'

He began to smile, then kissed her forehead carefully. 'You choose damn strange times to tell me things, Celeste. Or rather, not to tell me?'

'Nantes?' She picked up his meaning.

'Is it true what Bernard said? Did you sell yourself there to allow me to go free?'

'Yes.'

Already there were footsteps coming up the stairs and along the passageway, the noise of the contretemps attracting the attention of his staff. Within a second the door was opened, by Aurelian de la Tomber of all people, three of Shay's servants standing behind him.

His friend's eyes flickered over the carnage in the room. 'I had come to tell you Bernard has been spotted in London, but I see you already knew that. Are you going to live, Miss Fournier?'

'I am.'

'Good. Shay has been like a wounded bear since you parted in Nantes. It is time to resolve the troubles between you.'

Calling his man forward, he instructed him to fetch a physician promptly and then he turned towards Celeste.

'You were right in exposing Mattieu Benet, Mademoiselle Fournier, but I would like to give you my side of the story if I may...'

He waited until she nodded.

'The Ministry of War already had him in their sights. He'd been known to be unscrupulous and we needed to find solid proof. It was why I was there at the scene of the murder. We had word he was after Felix Dubois and I knew he was planning to leave Paris. I tried to protect the children, but I couldn't.'

Celeste was glad of his honesty, but she had some of her own also. 'It was my fault, too. The documents that were found on them came from me. The courier I sometimes used also worked for Mattieu Benet and he made sure that they were implicated.'

A new voice was heard outside and a physician stepped into the room.

'This man said I was to come immediately...' He gestured to the servant at his side, but his words dwindled to nothing as he saw Guy Bernard's body on the floor lying before them.

'It seems there is nothing at all I can do for the gentleman, but perhaps the lady might need my ministrations?'

'Thank you.' Shay stood and lifted Celeste up in his arms, ignoring completely her protests to be put down.

Aurelian turned to go. 'Then I shall retrieve my great-aunt, Shay. She has been in London visiting with her sister and you would be hard pressed to find two more proper Dowagers. Their presence in the house is important to protect the reputation of your young guest.'

Both he and Celeste looked over at him.

'Unlike Paris, London prides itself on the rigorous upholding of manners and decorum. We should not let the city down. Tante Adalicia and her sister will be in residence within the hour. It is my gift to you both.'

With various servants looking on and the doctor nodding his head vigorously, Shay had no way of insisting otherwise. He could only walk behind the procession of doctor and servants with Celeste in his arms as they led the way to the yellow bedchamber on the second floor of the Luxford town house.

She was finally alone.

All the prodding and stitching and bandaging had finished, the elixirs given, the candles lit, and beside her bed, well protected against the autumn cold, the old great-aunt of Aurelian de la Tomber sat, black shawl around her shoulders and drinking a generous brandy.

Celeste could hardly believe what had happened. Guy Bernard was dead, never to trouble her again, and Summer seemed to be having no trouble at all in digesting the fact that he'd killed him. She had also told him that he was beautiful in a way that would leave him with no doubt at all that she wanted more.

Her frown deepened for he had not replied or given her any compliment back. Granted, her timing was probably off, but still...

She looked across at Aurelian de la Tomber's aunt and smiled, a stretched parody of a smile, she supposed, because all she truly wanted was Summer here in her bed, here where she might touch him and kiss him and...

'My sister and I are quite elderly, Miss Fournier, and our usual retiring hour is long since reached, so I will bid you a good night. We both sleep very well and deeply and I hope that you shall, too.'

Celeste was not quite sure what the old lady was telling her.

'Viscount Luxford speaks French remarkably well for an Englishman. His accent is that of a perfect Parisian gentleman, though when my sister quizzed him on his time in Provence his speech took on the musicality of that part as well. A man of many talents, my dear. A good man.'

'He is.'

'Our chambers lie on the first floor to the very back of the house. Lian insisted that we take such rooms because of the many stairs. A most insistent man, my great-nephew. And wily, too. I sometimes wonder whether the darker arts might have been more his calling than the banking he is involved in. I said as much to his mother many times, but I doubt she ever told him.'

For a moment Celeste could not quite find her voice. 'Thank you for coming so quickly and on such short notice, *madame*.'

'Oh, it is my pleasure, Miss Fournier. Respectability has its uses, my dear, as does putting on a fine face. It is just as well that we were here to be of assistance.'

When she left, Celeste sat up. Her arm had been pulled into a sling, the cotton soft against her skin. A nightgown had been procured from somewhere, as had a night jacket and warm woollen slippers. A maid had combed her hair and tied it into a ribbon and she had been bathed in lilac water and rose oil, the soap of lavender adding its bit to the potpourri of toilettes.

All in all, she smelt like a flower shop, albeit an expensive one. It had been a very long time since she had felt so very pampered and coddled. Underneath all the shock she liked the feeling, although she knew on the morrow she would return to Langley.

It was over. Danger. The past. Retribution. She was safe. They were safe, she and Loring and Summer. The absolute relief of it all made her heart sing.

'Please God, let him come.'

She whispered this under her breath and was mindful of the quietening of the house around her: the last foot-falls of the servants, the clock on the mantel ringing out the early hour of morning, one plaintive note at a time.

Then the door handle moved and the door opened and Summerley Shayborne, Viscount Luxford, stood there, newly bathed himself, his necktie loose and with-out any sort of a jacket.

'May I come in?'

She nodded and he walked forward, holding a candle that was almost burned down to the wick.

He stopped a little distance from the bed, placing the candle down at her level on the small bedside table.

'Is your arm feeling better?'

'Much.' She could barely say more.

'Tell me about Nantes, Celeste. Let me hear the truth from you.'

'You do not think Guy Bernard had the way of it?'

'I don't know.'

'He did and he didn't. He didn't know that the only time I have ever felt honourable was when you were with me. He couldn't know that if you had died I would have, too, because seeing you safe was all I had left.'

'The agents of Les Chevaliers were at the port then and you spoke to them when I went to meet Aurelian?'

She nodded. 'There were five of them and they had been waiting for a week. Two of the older men held great ambitions to replace Benet, so my allegations whet their appetites for a regime change.'

'You knew that about them?'

'I made it my business to.'

'So you struck a deal with them? Your honesty for my safe passage?'

'Well, it was a little more complicated than that. You were right out in the open and one of the agents was the finest marksmen in all of France. He would not have cared if others were in the way and got hurt and I knew that he hated Aurelian de la Tomber with a passion.'

'So it was for both of us, then?'

'I decided to implicate de la Tomber, too, for if I could not save him in Paris, then at least I might try in Nantes and I had seen him outside the Dubois home just before the children were killed.'

'A fortunate happenstance?'

'I thought so. I promised I would accompany the agents back to Paris of my own free will and give my accusations when I got there, but I also insisted that I retained my weapons at hand. If anyone touched me, I would kill myself. They made certain no one did, for arriving empty-handed in Paris would have invited sterner questions than each thought they might survive.'

'And in Paris?'

'Well, things went a bit awry there because Benet is

wily and de la Tomber is clever. But I kept saying what I thought was true despite the opposition and within a day there was an inquiry.'

'And then you left?'

'Carefully at midnight on the third day, for everything I had set out to do was done and de la Tomber seemed to be safely absolved from it all.'

'A perfect outcome for everyone, save you?'

She smiled. 'It was the end of everything, anyway, and the resulting confusion made my escape easy.'

He shook his head and walked to the window, looking out with his hands on the sill. Then he turned.

'You told me today that I was beautiful, both inside and out. Was that something you have regretted saying since?'

A jolt of shock ran down from her throat to her stomach, making her breathless. He never had been a man to skirt about issues, but then, neither had she. 'It is not. I love you. I will always love you. For ever and ever.'

'God.'

'When you left the port safely and I watched the sails of your fishing boat fill with air as it made for the open sea, all I could think was, this is my finest moment. I had not lost you to death and there was still hope in life for us.'

'Us?' A new tone in his question held her still.

'I missed you and I hoped you might have missed me, too.'

'I did, every day.'

She watched him as he came forward to kneel on the thick Aubusson rug next to the bed, his hand searching for hers and taking it into his own, the fingers warm and strong.

'Will you marry me, Celeste? Will you do me the honour of becoming my wife?'

'Your wife?' She had never believed he would ask her this, never even hoped for it. Such a proposal was so far from any expectation that she was momentarily mute.

'My wife, to have and to hold for ever. In sickness and in health. For richer, for poorer.' He began to smile. 'In bed and out of it. In danger and in safety. In France and in England. In my heart and blood and soul. That sort of wife.'

'You were always good with words, Summer.'

'And you were always good at hiding, Celeste.'

'If I say yes, you might regret it, and besides, you have said nothing at all to me of love. I have to have that.'

'Have I not? Is it not here?' He touched their joined hands with his free one and then his fingers rested lightly on the bandage above her elbow. 'Or here?'

Celeste had the honesty to nod.

'I promise you faith and hope, but mostly I promise you love and the grace to stay exactly as you are.'

'And what am I, Summer? To you?'

'Everything,' he whispered and when his voice broke she was amazed. Here was a man who had saved armies and enabled countries to throw off the mantle of an unwanted ruler. A man who was a hero to one half of Europe and a hallowed enemy to the other. Yet he was promising her fealty. Her with her chequered past and a future that was uncertain, to say the least.

Everything.

She could not stop the tears falling as he kept talking.

'I love you so much that I have allowed Aurelian to place these ancient relatives in my home, precluding me from any sort of hope of luring you to my bedroom. I love you so much that I am prepared to wait until our wedding night to know again the utter joy I knew in France. I love you so much that I wish to do everything properly from now on.'

'Properly?'

'I will court you until I wear down any resistance to my proposal and you marry me out of love and lust.'

She smiled at that, but knew she could not capitulate completely.

'You must come with me to Langley on the morrow, for I have one last secret for you. A good one,' she added when she saw him frown. 'The very best.'

'And if I do this, will you give me your answer?'

She pulled his face into her hands and kissed him with all her heart, nothing hidden or held back.

'I will.'

'Then I shall hold you to it, but for now it's best if I am not here alone with you.'

He stood, tipping his head in a goodbye. Then he was gone.

'Please God,' she whispered, wiping away the tears. 'Please God, let me be good enough for him and let him love Loring.'

She was exhausted and her arm hurt, but the wonderment of her day danced over everything.

* * *

The tension between them was back as they drove south, all the confessions and high emotions from the night before quietened now into the reality of what they had nearly lost and what they still hoped to gain.

'Aurelian made certain Guy Bernard's body was dealt with. At least there won't be an official inquiry into it.'

Waking this morning, Shay had felt no remorse at all for killing the Frenchman, his knives poised to murder Celeste. He could never bother them again and Celeste appeared as relieved as he to have the threat dealt with and removed.

He wanted her to tell him that she loved him again. He wanted to kiss her and hold her and understand the magic that had never gone away in all the months that they were apart.

She had almost forfeited her life for his in Nantes. That gift alone told him everything he needed to know.

'Where did you go after leaving Paris?

'I went to Calais. It was large enough to get lost in, but small enough not to be lost to myself.'

There were things there in her expression that he wondered about. She had not gone to Italy and to the warmth, ease and beauty of a place where she had con-tacts. She had gone instead to the colder climes of the department of Pas-de-Calais. Nothing made sense.

She was fidgeting with her clothing, her fingers play-ing with the material in her old and worn-out trousers. She'd insisted on wearing the cloak on top as well and no amount of persuasion on his part would have her shed it. Hiding as usual. She was both nervous and desperate. He could read the emotions on her face.

As they came up the driveway to Langley, she leaned forward, watching the windows above the portico and positioning herself to move the second the conveyance came to a halt.

'Are you expecting someone?' He asked this because he so plainly could see that she was.

'When the carriage stops we will go into the house and straight upstairs. I have to tell you now. I don't want to wait.'

'Very well.'

He could not for the life of him understand what might be awaiting him but, if it was important to Celeste, then it would be important to him, too.

She smiled at his answer and for the first time since last night touched him gently on his hand.

'I am not mad or delusional or whatever you may be thinking. It will all be explained when we go upstairs. But we must hurry.'

The second the conveyance ceased moving she was out, hurrying for the front steps, the front door, the tall and winding staircase, a darker passage and then another door.

'Stay here for just a moment. Please.'

He heard quiet voices inside and then the door reopened and a maid scurried away, curiosity bathing her homely face as she glanced across to him.

A second later Celeste was there, her hand held out waiting for his.

'He needs to see us together.'

The cot was small and beautifully decorated with Brussels lace and the finest lawn. When she pulled back the blankets a child lay there watching them. A light-haired child with eyes the colour of his own and a nose and mouth that reminded him so forcibly of something he sought to put a name to.

The picture in his bedchamber in London. The one done in red chalk and fine lines. Himself as a small baby all those years before.

'He is ours, Summer. His name is Loring, which means son of a great warrior in old French. He is almost five months old.'

'My God.' He came closer and the movement had the baby's eyes following him. 'My son. Our son.'

'Yes.'

Happiness and joy were imprinted upon Celeste's face as she lifted him up and cradled the baby against her, one hand behind his head and the other tight beneath his bottom. She kissed his hair with reverence and relief and pure utter delight and then kissed him again.

'You restored my honour, Summer, and Loring restored my hope. So the answer to your proposal is, yes, we will marry you, if you can accept us together.'

At that he placed his arms about them, a circle of love and protection, a circle that would never be broken, not today, not tomorrow and not, God willing, in all the years of their marriage.

'I love you both, but I never expected a gift like this. A son. Our son.'

At that she handed the little bundle over, showing him how to hold up Loring's head and keep him safe.

Small fingers rose and clutched at his own, the nails with perfect crescents of white.

For the second time in two days he felt undone, he who in all his years of warfare had barely shed a tear.

It was the end of a long and lonely journey. He had finally come home.

Lady Faulkner met them as they walked down the stairs, her face alight with interest.

'Luxford?' Her glance went to their joined hands and then to the baby. 'He is the father, I presume?' She looked straight at Celeste. 'The resemblance is there for anyone with eyes to see.'

'He is, Grandmère, and it was not impossible, after all.'

At that, the years on the older woman's face fell away, the creases of tension softening.

'It could not be more marvellous,' she said finally. 'If I could have conjured up someone for my granddaughter, Summerley, the man on the top of the list would have been you.'

'Not just someone,' he said quietly. 'Celeste has consented to marry me as soon as we are able and I hope you will give us your blessing.'

'Then God has answered all my prayers and the sadness of Langley has been lifted for good. From now on there will only be wonderful times.' She stopped. 'At least until Loring grows up and begins to worry us with the taste for adventure he has most assuredly inherited. Then we will all have to take in a breath.' Stepping forward, she took his hand in her own. 'Your parents would have been pleased, Shayborne, and so would your grandfather, Celeste. Perhaps Mary Elizabeth, August and Jeremy will be looking down and smiling, too.'

'I hope so.'

Much later, Loring was asleep in his cot and the night outside was silent and dark. Although Summer had wanted to do everything properly, as he put it, Celeste had no more will to wait.

She wanted him now, inside her, making her feel everything she had always thought she never would again.

'Are you sure?'

His words entered the night as he slipped into the bed beside her, the warmth of his skin sending a blazing desperation through her.

'I am. But you will find me different.'

She kept the sheet knotted in her hands, anchoring the fabric under her chin.

'Different because you are now the mother of our son?'

'Childbirth is not an easy thing.'

'Let me look. Let me see you in the candlelight. Please.'

When she dropped the sheet he traced the small scars of childbirth that she knew crossed her hips and then his fingers rose up to the new curve at her breasts.

'It's why you did not want me to touch you in London?'

She could only nod.

'You are even more beautiful than I remember you to be and that is saying something. You are tempered in steel, but bathed, too, in honey, sweet and supple and soft, and I want you.'

Relaxing back after such a compliment, she looked straight at him.

'This time, Summer, we will make love from the fullness of our life. This time the future, not the past, will rule us.'

His hand fell lower as he leaned down to kiss her. 'This time, Celeste, it is for ever.'

She came to him bathed in faith and when the hardness of his sex drove into her centre, she shut her eyes and breathed. Always she had tried to fill the nothingness with a temporary dissolution of fear, a momentary escape.

Tonight she could only find the joining, the place where they ceased to exist separately and both became one. Tonight as a nightingale called from the tree outside the window, Celeste knew she would hear these sounds all of the years of her existence, their existence, hers and Summer's and Loring's and any other child with whom they might be blessed.

'I want lots of children,' she told him as the waves inside her heightened and he lost the power to hold back and came within her strong and deep and true.

'As many as you like. You are mine,' he said as her own release followed. 'For ever.'

As the moon rose he brought her a glass of white wine and they sat in the candlelight and talked.

'Why didn't you go to Italy, Celeste, to have our son?'

She took a large sip and leaned back. When she spoke she did not look at him.

'The pregnancy was difficult. I was so sick I simply could not face the thought of a long journey south, so I chose to travel north instead.'

'What happened?'

'I became sicker and finally a woman took me in. Eloise Mercier was her name and she was a healer. She had a way with natural herbs and made a living in administering medicines to those who were ill in the area.'

'And so you recovered with her help?'

'I did. It was so good being away from deceit and subterfuge and for a while I stopped glancing over my shoulder and looked inside instead. To Loring. I didn't have you, but I had him, and all I could hope was that he would be a child that might resemble his father so that I had a part of you left. But even then I knew that there would always be people who would want to harm me and I needed to keep Loring safe. So I wrapped him up in the warmest blankets I could find and took passage on a boat to England.'

'And returned to your grandmother?'

'Yes. I had no notion you would ever forgive me and I knew that you were probably a viscount to boot. It was a risk to return to Langley with Luxford so very close, but for Loring's sake it was one that I was willing to take.'

'I should have come looking for you. I nearly did many a time, but...'

'I'd run from you once already?'

'That and the fact that if I had tried to locate you,

it might have made everything far more dangerous for you.'

'Maybe it would have. When you cast out such a wide net it is never certain who might be caught within it.'

'Then I thank God that you and Loring are safe now and home.'

'Summer?'

'Yes?'

'I'd like our wedding to be here at Langley with only a handful of guests. Grandmère. Vivienne Shayborne and perhaps Aurelian de la Tomber? Do you think that is something you might want as well?'

'I'll get a special licence and send word to Lian tomorrow. If all goes to plan, we can be married within three days.'

Epilogue

One year later—London

The Barrymore Ball was the talk of the Season, with its colourful interiors, its unusual cuisine and its musicians who were the very cream of Europe's talent.

No expense had been spared and the place was full of people. Rich people. Interesting people. Bohemian people. People who looked as though they were neither interesting nor rich, but were there to enjoy the present. A melting pot of people in a setting that was unmatched.

'I did not imagine that the English could rival even the greatest of the Parisian soirées.' Celeste almost had to shout these words. 'But I think this one just might.'

'You went to such occasions with your father?'

She shook her head. 'I peeked a few times into the Tuileries Palace whose high windows on both sides of the building can be scaled easily if you know how. I thought the women were like princesses.'

'You look like one tonight, the most beautiful princess of them all.'

She used her fan in the way she had observed other women here wielding theirs and hoped she had covered her blush. Marriage suited her, she loved the endless days and nights in her husband's company at Luxford and the intimacy of their connection.

'Look at me like that for much longer and I will have to take you home again, my darling, to enjoy in privacy what your eyes are promising.'

She was on the point of agreeing when their names were called, the ringing tones of the major-domo loud above the crowd.

'Viscount and Viscountess Luxford.'

In all the months they had been married, she had never got over the thrill of hearing their names linked, though when the chatter died down and hundreds of faces turned their way she had a moment of disquiet.

If anyone recognised her…

But even she could barely see the old her in the new one any more. She was happy and in love, a wife and a mother, a granddaughter and the chatelaine to a house more stately than any she could ever have imagined. The furtive, careful Mademoiselle Brigitte Guerin had been replaced by a far more certain Lady Luxford, for with Summer at her side she knew she was loved.

An hour later she saw Aurelian de la Tomber thread his way towards them with a smile on his face.

'You are most assuredly the belle of the ball, Celeste,'

he said when he finally reached them. 'And I can see the chagrin on all the mamas' faces, Shay, as they realise you are off the market.'

Aurelian had come up to Luxford to be the best man at their wedding and Celeste had enjoyed his company as much as Shay had, though she had made a point to apologise to him for her accusations in Paris.

He'd waved such a confession off completely and moved into a house not even an hour down the road in Sussex to be nearer them, a beautiful old manor that he'd had remodelled.

The gown Celeste wore shimmered under the light of the chandeliers, enhancing the shot-blue silk with shards of silver. When she had put it on she had thought it was the most beautiful dress she had ever seen.

'Will you dance with me, my love?' Summer's grip tightened as the first strains of the waltz were in evidence. Excusing themselves, they made their way through the throng of people to the dance floor where everything felt magical.

'I told you that you would be unmatched and you are. Every man here is looking at you as though he would like to kiss you. Or more.'

'I think you are addled, Summer. It's you all the girls are ogling.'

When he smiled he brought her in against his body, so that she could feel the outline of him, hard and tight, the music flowing about them. As the dance progressed and his eyes bored into her own she knew he was asking her things that belonged in the bedchamber and not here in society, and there was an excitement that welled inside her at the forbidden.

'Yes,' she whispered and pushed against him. 'Yes,' she said again as the hardness grew.

She watched him swallow, but the gleam in his eyes was dangerous. 'Take care, my sweet. Play with fire and you shall be burned.'

'Do you promise?'

His amber eyes were predatory and she shivered in delight, glad when the music finished and he took her hand in his and led her from the room.

Once in the carriage he brought her up on to his lap and kissed her in the way that made her heart and soul sing.

'You were the most beautiful woman in the room to-night, Celeste, and any doubt you held of belonging in the *ton* must surely be long gone. They love you. I have had a dozen invites to other balls across the next fortnight.'

'But we won't stay, will we? You promised we would go home tomorrow to Luxford.'

'Absolutely. But at least we have the choice now of coming back.' He looked out the window and frowned. 'This ride home is interminable and the fire you started back there is burning me up.'

When she laughed he held her tightly against him, pleased to see the town house finally coming into view.

After the fire came the quiet and he played with her hair, twirling the curls in the moonlight around one finger.

'It's so much longer now. When I first met you I

wondered about the true colour, for you wore so many other shades.'

She laughed. 'The white wig? It was so horribly noticeable and it was expensive. I only wore it that once.'

A cry from the door had them turning, the small figure of Loring appearing in the moonlight, a blanket in his arms.

'Come, sweetheart,' he said and pulled back the covers, a soft warm bundle of boy climbing in. 'We are here so there is no need to be afraid.'

Shay loved holding his son. He loved his smallness and the way he was changing, and as he had missed out on the first months of his life he did not plan to be absent for a moment more. That included the nighttime, even though Celeste scolded him for allowing their son into bed.

He was a toddler now with all the inherent busyness and danger. Yesterday Shay had found him at the top of the wide staircase and his heart had leapt into his throat with fifty times the force it ever had in the heat of Europe's battles. There were two maids caring for him and even that number never quite seemed to be able to contain him.

Lady Faulkner always regaled them with stories of Shay's own daring childhood whenever Loring escaped or fell or had a tantrum, and Celeste loved to hear them.

Family.

It was growing by the day.

Celeste. Loring. Susan Joyce. Vivienne. Aurelian. Even Celeste's reclusive uncle was becoming less shy and withdrawn. And now a new little child due in the summer. He hoped this one would be a daughter with blonde hair and eyes that changed with her emotions exactly as her mother's did.

'I was often lonely and now I think I might never be so again.' He said this with a smile, but Celeste answered seriously.

'In Paris I thought I might die from isolation. If I had, it would have been the very worst death possible.'

'Well, my love, there is no danger of that ever happening with our growing brood.'

She stretched and gave a sigh. 'I want five children, Summer. Or six. But if all our offspring are invited to share our bed, then how are we to make more?' She left it open as a question.

He leaned down to kiss her and their son did, too, and he smiled as she opened her arms and placed them warmly about them both, gathering them in.

* * * * *

If you enjoyed this story you won't want to miss these other great Regency reads by Sophia James:

*RUINED BY THE RECKLESS VISCOUNT
A SECRET CONSEQUENCE FOR THE VISCOUNT*

And if you enjoy these books check out Sophia's
THE PENNILESS LORDS *quartet,*
starting with

MARRIAGE MADE IN MONEY